VonBrutal

By Cyndi O'Hara

Dedicated to Carol Conrad

who is a lover of literature

and the most supportive and

encouraging individual that I know.

Chapter 1

April 1939 was one of the few months when not many major events transpired in Nazi Germany. Although the rains were crisp and fogy, there seemed to be a short reprieve before the Nazi war engine reconvened for the onward laughter of an evil empire. Maybe the think-tank was out of ideals for control and destruction, or maybe they were living the good-life as superior Arians at parties with all the power that men could possess between their loins. Events—in other words, atrocities—still occurred, but on a smaller scale and less recognized. The unfortunate who were still citizens of Germany were in danger of losing their lives and everything they had ever worked for during a lifetime besides hopes, dreams and aspirations.

The year began in January as that usually does with the commencement of any calendar. Hitler threatened the Jews during his Reichstag speech which embarked the outbreak of war and the trial run for the New World Order. This would be the catalyst to the liquidation of the Jews who were targeted as enemies of the Reich for the soul reason being, they were the only successful people in Nazi Germany. There was much the Reich was to steel from them, especially their insurance policies backed by the Vatican. By March, Czechoslovakia was taken over by the Nazis, and they wrapped up their military efforts with their slaughter in the Spanish Civil War. Times were precarious, and life had little value, especially for those who were not part of the "In Crowd". A dark tide had turned black as the deepest abyss. This epoch was in favor of those of a darker nature where the devil was on the ground; those who found their opportunity, power, and position in the world at the expense of others.

On the first of April, the misty morning moistened the long jet-black hair of Frans VonBrutal. He was not a joking sort of guy when he loaded up his motorcycle. The incredible BMW R75 came equipped with a sidecar that he utilized for the belongings of a man on a mission, and the side car was to hold a case of Jägermeister. This was a popular beverage, and the name translated to "hunting master," which he was in every sense of the definition of his disposition in life. The lovely drink Jägermeister was also referred to in terms as Herrmann Göring's schnapps, because the office of Göring was also affiliated with hunting licenses. Frans thought he had that sort of connection to that guy.

Frans stuffed his grayish wool bedroll between the side seat and his box of Fatherland booze. He did not want the liquor to get damaged during his thousand-mile adventure to Sofia, Bulgaria which would have the unthinkable and the ultimate waste. In Sofia, he would have work to do by extracting information by any means possible for the Reich which needed pertinent information. Frans packed his hand tools along with dental instruments and an assortment of razors, sharp knives. He anticipated with glee the killing with torturing he would do along with the employment of anyone he could find to utilize in his endeavors. Yet he felt perturbed that he'd been commissioned to receive so little funds for his work—just sustenance pays for his expertise. Many of Fran's cohorts worked for ideology as rewards besides a liter full of German beer for serving the greater cause of the Reich.

VonBrutal continued loading his sidecar. Frans held on to one pack of Neune Front, lighting one smoke and tucking the rest of the pack in the inner pocket of his long black leather trench coat. His clothing gave him an even more ominous presence, as that jacket gleamed in the light but reeked of death. Then VonBrutal reminisced about how the same manufacturer of smokes, Sturm-Zigaretten, had sold Trommler, a brainchild of Otto Wagener who was the economic adviser and confident to Adolf Hitler. This was to raise funds for the Nazi Sturmabteilung who provided protection at rallies some years earlier. The guy was planning when he purchased numerous packs of tobacco and fuel for his pure-silver lighter which had a skull emblazoned on it. While tucking everything away, he finished the cigarette and tossed the butts on the ground in his neighbor's yard.

As he looked up at the sky, VonBrutal saw the grandiosity of his future. His pasty white face smiled an evil grin. He thought, "What a wonderful day to start with for abject espionage." The weather was clear as any beautiful day could be even though the air had a dampening chill of early spring. Frans kick-started his cycle and gave it time for the engine to warm up as he went back into his home to grab his toolbox for the road. He checked for provisions, but never bothered to pack food. Soon enough VonBrutal realized that his wife Heidi did not remind him of his appetite. Grabbing what available food there was which composed of the diner the night before, he looked on for the bag of oatmeal and bottles of water along with a pound of butter and some salt.

The two had been married some 10 years earlier. VonBrutal and his wife lived in Berlin with their two children, Ella who was 12 and Sara was 7. Of course, Frans met his precious Heidi during an evening of intense drinking. Their romance was love at first sight even though she was of a lower class. He loved the sway of her hips and obvious footwear. Some time had passed in their marriage when she confided in him that she'd blown five storm troopers the night before she met him during a party where she was the center of attention. That night Heidi was paid as entertainment. She did not seem to care until Frans's sadistic side emerged as his dual personality was unpredictable and felt the violence of his ways. At moments, the man was sweet and caring, but then he would turn medieval in a split second. Frans became sexually aroused when he inflicted pain on others. His energy changed as his face contorted; he could kill in a second, and felt he had the divine right to do so as he was a creature of both heaven and hell. VonBrutal was the ultimate judgment, authority and hangman. Or, so he thought. Heidi was financially unable to leave Frans because her beauty had faded quickly, and the likelihood of attaching herself to another male supporter was not probable. Heidi did not age well. She at least had that gist of reality yet did not care she married into a powerful family that had complicated dynamics and utter distain for her. There was something else that kept her in this abusive relationship: Frans was so good in bed as a divine lover. He was very good in bed with almost supernatural talents that brought a woman to euphoria. That was why she tolerated Herr VonBrutal's violent rampages because he gave her the best sex, she'd ever had even though she knew she could lose her life at any moment. Heidi thought sometimes, "I cannot believe that this is my life." The woman was trapped with no options to speak of which was not so uncommon beside that was the norm. There was no Prince Charming on the horizon to rescue his fair princess otherwise known as the damsel in distress. Was that because chivalry was dead or was Heidi just a gutter rat?

Heidi had been a nightclub entertainer because she was very beautiful, although she was not that charming when she spoke. Her speech was laced with unsophisticated words and derogatory, impulsive expressions that would take one back in offence. She worked in a club called Das Hornhause, where she wore revealing costumes and performed burlesque routines along with dancing and singing. Having a killer body was what got her by, because she had no talent to speak of. She was all but a curvy disposition with a tight midline. Her hair was long and provocative, yet not often washed her mane. The main point with her work was that she could not sing, nor could she dance; she could only flaunt her body. Patrons would often invite her over to their tables so that she earned drink commissions. She would soon joyfully help the customers out in a room behind the stage. The guys afterwards remarked of what a great deep throater Heidi was because without reservation she was able to inhale a man's whole cock in entirety down her throat and suck him dry. The gal had gifts beyond all means.

Somehow, which was strangely transpired, VonBrutal fell in love with his precious as if he was at an oasis in the deserts in Saudi Arabia. Heidi was his vision of grandeur, beauty and womanhood. He had to have her at that given time to consume her. Thus, Herr VonBrutal spoke with the house manager Jörg at Das Hornhause. VonBrutal said, "I have to have her; she is my light. My heart pounds for her."

Jörg was quite taken aback that the man wanted a prostitute for his wife. This guy had been running Das Hornhause for over 20 years. He had no respect for the girls expect the legal tender that his workers brought in for financial gain. Heidi even sucked Jörg many times over on his command which made Jörg quite content. The question VonBrutal posed took Jörg a few minutes to respond to. Jörg interjected, "If you want her for a date, you must cough up a certain amount of Marks, and for a permanent resolution would be considerably more." He thought what a deranged man VonBrutal was to demand such a request.

VonBrutal saw himself as a big spender. He pulled a wad of cash out of his pocket, and paid Jörg with the money his father had given him as an allowance. There were years of insanity that followed the acquisition of his desired. Dishes were broken, and VonBrutal punched holes in the walls of the house because he owned the house through his father's good will. As a response, VonBrutal said to Heidi, "I'm doing this because we will be here forever by living and dying in this house together!" In all actuality, the house had been a gift from his father as a wedding present, Herr VonBrutal Sr who was deeply rooted in the Nazi movement and the best of buddies with those in the hierarchy. The family had been stunned when he married Heidi, because she was such a slut. Even VonBrutal's sisters, Danu and Daria, were taken aback, and had a very difficult time being cordial to Heidi. They did not know how to handle the complicated family dynamics, nor did Danu and Daria have a choice. All were to play along with the scenario. Things got worse when she had Ella out of wedlock then a few years latter Sara was born. The VonBrutal family cringed.

The day came when Heidi was glad to see Frans go. *Finally!* Finally, she thought, she would get lucky and never be obliged to see him again. She knew that she could find male companionship elsewhere as she had from the past.

That glorious day! Frans took his time riding out of Berlin. He marveled at how he had such a minacious presence and grandeur. He looked good at that point. He was at the height of his manliness, or so he believed. As he passed storefront windows with swastikas painted on the glass, he was pleasured from seeing his own reflection in its entirety. He was not blond, but he was a beaming example of the Aryan nation, a marvel with his chiseled looks and strong physical stature. Molded from the essence of superiority, he ordained himself as perfection, and was in awe of his manhood. VonBrutal was widely accepted in the Nazi community and had many associates. None of them were friends. Focused now, he rode south towards Prague where he would spend the night with no worries nor a care in the world and have cocktails with an old friend. Frans knew himself as a Nazi demigod from the blackest pit of hell or as an immortal. The power surged through his veins which was a fiery animalistic instinct. He could not wait to unleash the demon bottled inside his core.

A month prior to this, Hitler had annexed Czechoslovakia. Immigrants from Germany were taken back. Their save haven was lost. Thus, VonBrutal's rolling into Prague was easy for any German to do. The way was paved. The citizens had no idea what was to hit them. Many despicable atrocities were to come.

The motorcycle escapade was a working vacation with much in store because Frans had his wings. He had the feeling that he could fly when he was riding. He would soon soar with his newfound identity which was to transform him. Frans intended to fulfill each attribute he possessed. No matter how derogatory his stance was, he was a man on the move with approval from the Reich to utilize his talents to the utmost.

Frans enjoyed the countryside and its meandering roads. Of course, he wore an eye protection underneath his goggles because he was blind in his left eye. The feeling from the rush of air coming over him was a true delight. He felt different beyond what any human being could ever grant him because he held a sense of inflated ego. VonBrutal made stops frequently at any interesting outpost where people were gathered. There were nights when he rested at taverns that were well-lit from the road inviting him in. He pounded the drinks and harassed the other patrons. VonBrutal also insulted the bartenders, because he was a predator which was how he saw himself. He wanted all the bar music to suit him exclusively.

Along the road was nothing different then was to take place in the blackened tavern in Prague so he thought. That night there was a thunderstorm, and water ran everywhere. Soaking wet and cold, he had a rendezvous. VonBrutal's father had an old acquittance he wanted his son to meet with by the name of Herr

Tötung who was a fabulous sort of elegant German warlord that associated with Nazi bikers. His dynasty dated back to the Roman times. And, that dude was quite handsome with striking features, and his eyes were dark and mysterious encompassed by silver long hair pulled tight at the nap of his skull. Tötung was quit a divine alpha male with an eluding sex appeal. As VonBrutal walked in, Tötung already had their drinks, and quickly gave a toast to the devil by saying, "I hope the trip there will be as pleasurable as the stay in Hell."

He then added, "How was your trip so far, and are your balls soar?"

VonBrutal interjected, "My balls are fine, yet I only killed two on the list so far." Then they smiled and drank their beers and shots. "This city is quite clean and beautiful."

Tötung, "Keep a heads up when you come across the Americans in Sophia. A keynote is that they like women. Let's drink some more."

This transpired for hours the drinking and conversation. VonBrutal lost his head. Then his host ask him if he ever tasted human blood. Tötung had a strange yellowish golden tint gleaming in his eyes and a devilish smirk. Then he said, "it tastes quite warm with a sweet bite."

VonBrutal replied, "No, I have not."

Tötung, "Would you like too?"

A creepy door opened in the back of the peaceful tavern and the two gentlemen got up and went through. They descended a flight of rickety stairs to a damp stinky urine filled basement with black mold everywhere and a dismal light hanging from the ceiling. The light seemed to flicker in and out giving a surreal effect of light and shadows dancing on the walls. There in an obscured corner tied up in a rickety old chair was a man with a burlap sack over his head, and a rope tied tightly around his neck that rope was extended firmly to a putrid dripping pipe on the ceiling. The victim had cloth stuffed in his mouth to prevent any utterance of objections of what was to occur. Beside the fact he was completely restrained, he had a ratty old wool blanket draped over his naked body.

Something evil was to transpire that evening. The Devil was present with a laughter that reeked though the air, and on the ground. His demons were all about planting scenarios in the heads of the perpetrators. This was to be an initiation ceremony into the pack, and VonBrutal heard a bizarre music box in somewhere of surreal distance that gave him goosebumps with the twanging nauseating sound. Four feet away was a nightstand with a silver four-sided dagger properly weighted by the intense handle with a metal spear on the end. This weapon had the means to penetrate a skull with one blow along with other implications or usefulness.

Tötung said, "let's begin."

With the tip of the dagger, Tötung began with some petite and gentle bloodletting of the juggler vein and main arteries of the subject's legs. The blood decanted onto the floor. Then Tötung began to drink from the openings that life blood was flowing through which seemed to have a stinky odor. He lapped up the red sangria like a dog at a trough. This seemed to give him an orgasmic pleasure, and his disposition changed to an aggressive sort. Tötung became more of an animal of a darker nature followed by grunting sounds and snorts with an objectively motivated vision to control VonBrutal as his prentice.

Tötung asked VonBrutal, "do you know what we are doing here?"

The response from VonBrutal was primal. Tötung did not notice at first how excited his guest was becoming. VonBrutal's mouth was watering with a foolish appetite, and his eyes were dilated. His root chakra was intensely opening, and he seemed hungry very hungry. With that, he swooped in, and drank fiercely from the victim's jugular vein filling himself up with the savory flavors. Then VonBrutal rested on his knees with the blood rolling down his cheek.

Tötung interrupted as he pointed to the weaponry on the stand, "time for you to finish the job boy."

VonBrutal took the dagger without hesitation and plunged it into the head of the victim. An odd smell poured out. A warmth came over him. His senses became heightened. VonBrutal's cojones enlarged tremendously with a grandiose weight. The hair on his neck stuck up along with the rest of his body hair that seemed to grow including his grown and around his anus. His mouth was painful as if he was teething. Most of all he slobbered so tremendously that the salivation streamed on to the dirt floor of the cellar making a puddle of drool. VonBrutal smacked his lips together as if he was hungry. There seemed to be little sparkles flying through the air coupled by dark glooms prowling in the corners of the drafty misty stank of urine. This was a heaven verse hell euphoria for VonBrutal who was grossly inclined into becoming the animal he was intended to be.

Then, Tötung removed the sac from the body's head. The countenance was that of abject agony with contorted features and mucus dripping throughout its face. VonBrutal saw no connection until Tötung announced that was Fran's father. Although, VonBrutal was not that taken back. He seemed to have an evil grim of satisfaction of killing the old man.

Tötung interjected ever so casually as he gave VonBrutal a hug, "Some of us will live to the end of all times, and then there are those who are disposable. Most are for the waste of the nonessential units. Your father served his purpose, yet he was not of the pack. This will become evident in time."

As shocking as that was, VonBrutal's reaction was that of vindication. That was a long time coming. He only wished he tortured the old man more before he was to get back on the road. VonBrutal Sr. was a controlling source because of that took his son's childhood away. Yes, Frans was given money and privilege. Yet, every Christmas he never got what he wanted besides a "Goddam Fucking Christmas Sweater" that was as ugly to lay one's eyes on. The old man was oppressive. So oppressive was VonBrutal Sr. that he raped Fran's sisters. The father killed VonBrutal's brother because Alrick who wanted to break free from the clan. Alrick was in love with a woman that worked for his father's business. The young man was uncomfortable with his arranged marriage with a woman that provided him no consortium. He sought affection elsewhere. Alrick thought he would go to Bavaria with his lover of his heart desire, yet he was found dead on the motorway thrown off from his BMW motorcycle. That was the sad truth. Frans was devastated at the loss of his brother as any man could morn such a devastation to a manly disposition. When men lose their brothers, there is no turning back. The pain never dissipates which stays for their lifetimes. Otherwise Frans had no love loss with his father, and glad to see the old man dead and decomposing. Yet, even though Frans was such a menace his father never killed him because he had absolutely no expectation on him. Frans was merely an annoyance and was always going under the wire "in order to" not be noticed for being so absurd.

Not more than a few minutes had passed VonBrutal felt a surge in his veins and his senses became in overdrive. He felt his heart pounding and his cojones enlarged even more as a grandiose exhibit. The hair on his arms and legs began to tingle and grow. Frans could not speak, but he grunted and growled. Then he dropped on all four and started chewing on the dead body of his father.

Then Herr Tötung pulled VonBrutal off the dead courps, and said, "down boy."

From VonBrutal's chewing and his face was bloody. His mentality was of a different realm. He seemed to be in a metaphysical high. Such an orgasmic pleasure was the greatest for him.

Herr Tötung statement, "Down boy; compose yourself. You do not seem to understand what was transpiring. Frans, everything is going to different from this day forward." The words curled off his lips sounding like an evil laughter. Tötung seemed to beam with joy. The old man was no longer useful to the Reich, yet Frans was the prodigy who would be of the most useful worker.

When VonBrutal finally departed from the horror scene, time passed, and so it did as time usually dose. As he scooted through Hungary nearing close to the border of Romania, a primal drive emerged, and he got a hard on. This was because he was partying it up in Czechoslovakia by making new friends, yet VonBrutal was killing some of them who were trusted by him. He had about a week's worth of riding through the countryside and valleys because he did not want to move his scooter up mountains. The terrain was breathtaking and majestic. The trees were budding, and the air was sweet with all that life could offer. Most nights, he slept under the stars like a cowboy. He plopped on his bedroll on the ground and drifted off into drunken oblivion. As he smoked his cigarettes, VonBrutal would flutter off to sleep, leaving the cigarette to burn its way through his blanket. Only upon awakening did he realize the catastrophe that had happened of his burnt up blankie.

      The world was alive, and he somehow stepped out of his evil ingrained nature for a brief moment and felt the connection to nature. Riding was his freedom and escape. This was how he got relief from his tormented twisted mind. Most of all he hated his father but had the pleasure of reconciling that situation. His mother was who she was that never spoke up against his father because of abject fear. Frans received many beatings, especially as a little boy. Mr. VonBrutal Sr. went about life making money by any means possible within the Weimar Republic. That meant that he made things happen. Disappearances were the old man's specialty. His father was one of the few men who were not Jewish to accumulate wealth which he did so unscrupulously. This was all in the name of making Marks. And, VonBrutal had his day that changed him forever.

Frans crossed over to the province of Transylvania, an area within Romania that had a colorful and bloody history. This made him think of the history of the land. How glorious a past Transylvania had, which intrigued his mind and very being. That was the homeland of Vlad the Impaler, who fought off the Ottoman Turks in the 1400s. For whatever sick reason, Vlad loved to watch the invaders die as their bodies were impaled on stakes. Their pain and screams enticed him as they slowly slid down on the Impaler's stakes. The weight of their bodies made their pierced bodies slide through the stakes. Vlad the ruler drank their blood by soaking it up with freshly baked bread. This guy was completely a sadist. Imagine the orgasmic sexual joy he felt from watching his victims in abject agony. Frans loved thinking about those gory endeavors. Obviously, there was something wrong with Frans.

The twisted path he took wove around the edge of the Hoia Baciu Forest as he neared Cluj-Napoca, Romania. This was the most haunted forest in the world. The time was nearing night, but he marveled at the twisted trees, the skanky smell in the air, and the creepiness of the whole scene. Frans felt rather at home and elated. There was an evil joy in his heart that warmed him. He thought to himself that his career as an SS officer, the Schutzstaffel, was right up his alley. He was part of the foremost power organization in Germany for surveillance and projecting terror. Being in the SS division called the Gestapo was a turn-on for his sadistic nature because he liked to hurt people. The Gestapo's purpose was to detect "any and all" targets who were a threat to the Reich. He thought his father, who was a German elitist, had the utmost pride in him, but not really. Frans was more of a perplexing bad child.

Somehow, Frans VonBrutal still wanted to think "be connected" with God strangely enough. He saw Jesus as his savior and lord. He even wore a blackened crucifix around his neck. Often, when he felt moved with anything spiritual. He would even become sullen and weepy at inspirational points. The few times (namely, three times) in which he went to Sunday service, when he walked through the doors, he heard the voice of God. God said to VonBrutal, "*Get out of my house.*" Trembling with humiliation, Frans would always stagger away in awe, and frazzled by the divine connotation that he could not go into a house of worship. He was born damned, and never had a spiritual chance in life. Being an evil sort of creature was strange for him, because if he could have, he would have walked with God. Yet, he could not change his nature, but he had the intelligence to know that what he was doing was wrong. There were no disputes: he was in a poor scenario either way.

Down the road he went off to great and exciting endeavors. He scooted towards new directions and mental thought. Soaring high was all that was to transpire. The loud exhaust pipes of his motorcycle reverberated in the air, and he was in soon-to-be conquered territories. VonBrutal thought to himself, "Am I alone here?" He pulled over to the side of the road, where there were many fallen branches that were dry and in a state of decay. So, Frans built a small and incredibly smoky fire that he intended to make big—"really big." In between his fire-making endeavor, he took swigs of one of his bottles of Jägermeister polishing one after another. Frans was camped in a rather dense patch of forest as he felt the presence of entities, dark shadow people and sprit creatures of the Transylvanian forest. As Frans drifted into oblivion with delightful dreams that composed two valleys one of elves and the other of dwarfs. Both were preparing for war. The elves war was not in contrast to the dwarfs, but towards the darker essence. The point was that these creatures were just defending themselves.

There was a resounding coming from the woods which made the madman erupt from his slumber. Then Frans heard when he began to focus that the sound was the howling of a pack of wolfs. This guy identified with k-9's which of whom embraced his heart in all sincerity. They sounded like music to his deranged mind, besides the fact he had a passion for music because that was the ultimate distraction, so he did not have to look at himself. Their howls seemed to dance in the air with the wolves' version of vocal songs. VonBrutal reminisced about some of his favorite nightclub tunes that he'd heard in person, which now brought him to orgasm. Frans howled back on all fours while arching his body toward the moon. He stared that moon down that night, as if Frans the Great were in control of the universe. What else was there to do on a full moon in a haunted forest where there were many trapped, tormented souls who lingered among the trees because these souls were murdered by ancient battles? The sounds seemed to enclose him—not just those of the wolves, but of the forest itself was beckoning. One brave wolf came to the edge of his campfire, growling and snarling and baring its teeth. The animal had a full and thick main. Frans got down on all fours again and growled and snarled back. This went on for quite some time as the evening passed. The wolf neared, and as it did, the demented man grabbed its furry coat and VonBrutal bared his teeth. The wolf licked Frans's teeth like a docile puppy. In this strange ritual, the wolf was acknowledging that Frans was the alpha male, which made Frans feel quite profound. He had done this with other dogs before, but never with a wolf. Being in touch with his animal nature took Frans to the astral plane which was the subconscious realm that went to inner existence. Abruptly, VonBrutal unrobed, and on all fours his body changed, he ran with the pack of wolves up and down the terrain smelling everything in reach. The wolves howled and so did he. When he came back to camp, he curled up with the wolves, and slipped into a peaceful oblivion on his bedroll completely naked.

WHEN HE AWOKE FROM HIS SLUMBER, the wolves were gone, and his fire was nothing but embers. The air was still, yet misty. He marveled at how good his motorcycle looked on a patch of moss, and what a man he was. Getting up to take a leek by a group of trees was a staggering endeavor. Then, he saw a hawk flying overhead. Taking that as a good luck scenario, he started his day's journey. His whole trip involved which path to follow the low roads through the valleys of the Balkan Mountains. The realization came that he had lost track of time and did not remember how many days had passed— nor did he really care. He loved riding and feeling the rush of air over his body as he blazed down the road fluttering his biker wings. He would get to Sofia when he would get there. He knew that the SS command saw him as a golden boy, so he thought he had free range to do whatever he wanted and so he did. The slow trip would give him time to find a hostage—preferably a young female—whom he intended to utilize in every sense of the word. Frans had to get out of that damned forest first if he could only find the way out which would take some time and find a main road that would lead to Cluj-Napoca. The wondering and misconceptions of reality or lack of direction went on way too long. The path seemed to clear after the Jägermeister was dissipated. It was all gone by then.

As usual, hunger was overcoming his stomach with a twisting, knotting pain, because he ran on fumes for weeks with nothing but alcohol and smokes. He did not think he was very much farther from town, so on he went. After this notion, he realized that gulping down some more Jägermeister was no longer an option. The herbs in the drink would have been substance alone.

Two hours later that very same day, the SS officer rolled into Cluj-Napoca on his motorcycle; he felt relaxed with his thighs opened, and that the whole face of the planet was in his grasp. He was the man. Control was at his beckon call. Even though he was dressed down he felt his sexual ominous presence; his full black leather coat was riddled with mud along with his boots from road splash. Mud was in his hair. There was a connotation of his threating character that he projected of sheer dark terror, yet this very outcome might not be disastrous. Although, his sexual allure was finely tuned VonBrutal was vigilant. Women love bad boys which he always said to Heidi. He searched his surroundings. Maybe that night he was to sleep in a room and have a shower. Strangely enough, he projected no body odor nor did he ever. Maybe that was how he could enter rooms undetected when his victims were right there for him to kill. He was a good individual in all clandestine matters; he was evil in an unspoken way. The unaware never saw nor sensed him coming, as Frans was a hound of hell.

With his dark penetrating eyes, he surveyed the streets, which were nearly empty. And Frans looked for a place to go inside for some easy access. So, once again his existence penetrated another drinking establishment was a dive bar, primarily that served up warm food and booze. He hoped for most of all some split tail because his radar was on, and he could smell sweet pussy from outside.

While VonBrutal assented the four steps to the entrance of the tavern he kicked off the mud from one boot to another on each inclination. Once he got to the door, he shook his leather trench coat as his he was shaking his skin fiercely like a primal beast. He pulled off his road goggles and stuck them in his pocket. Standing there and breathing for a moment, he searched for money with his nostrils undulating. Frans wanted to go in, but something made his hesitation. The shades were drawn and there was no view in sight. Ultimately, he waltzed in as the man he was taking up the establishment with his entire aura.

Frans sat down there at the counter for twenty minutes, with no service, no food, and no alcohol. He could have been infuriated, yet strangely he was not. He was relaxed and cordial. This continued until a young woman not much older than nineteen came to where he was sitting. His attitude shifted profoundly to be on point. The lights went on. There before him was this beautiful young woman with the smile of an angel. She was a breath of fresh air. Frans was not used to that type of woman. That perplexed him. For the moment, he was beside himself, holding his member in his pants. Her light-brown hair cascaded over her shoulders, and her cleavage was ever so alluring. He was fascinated with her milky white skin. And, her eyes were the most intriguing shade of blue, and then he thought, "Are her eyes green or are they blue?" When she walked away, her ass made him gasp for air. That woman had something beyond belief. And, the smell of her drove VonBrutal insane. She was fresh rain on a hot June day with the essence of flowers. He sensed how soft her skin was. Her dress laid upon her body ever so perfectly and across her shoulders.

VonBrutal undid the elastic from his long jet-black hair. Shaking it out, bits of mud flew landing some on the counter. He quickly wiped his hand on the counter tumbling the bits of mud to the floor. Running his hair through his hair, he smiled ever so alluring. His eyes looked perplexed as he surveyed the young lady. He could barely speak. That was not his nature to be so docile yet to be intrigued beside infatuated by her. The utterance came abruptly and friendly, "hello, my love. Tell me your name."

"Gilda." Then she said no more until she saw the swastika pins on his collar. Firmly, she wanted to ask, but did not. She thought, "What do you want from me?"

VonBrutal thought, "Make love with you. What else? Now, get me some beer and food!"

Annoyed, as if she could read his thoughts replied in her mind, "Fuck you! Anyway, I will bring you the ham and cabbage and a huge liter glass of beer for you to drown in you piece of shit!"

He smiled after reading her thoughts. She went to get him food.

She took her time serving him. When she finally did, she plopped all the meal down and intentionally spilled the beer on his ham and cabbage with a chuckle. Yet for what reason Gilda acted playful because she liked VonBrutal and was teasing him. That was all done with a courteous backwoods' tavern smile. In all actuality, she made him wait for his beer and food for a long time...a very long time. Yet he did not seem to care he was her elder of almost ten years older and knew the slyness of female counterparts. There were not more than a few patrons in the establishment. She did not care, and her attitude was that Nazis were not welcomed in that neck of the woods. Everyone knew full and well what was coming. She was just grateful that she was not Jewish and had some Aryan blood in her, since this would save her life for a time.

VonBrutal's energy changed in a less than a split second. Then with an open-handed slap to Gilda's face, he interjected, "My, my,..my! Don't you have an attitude with your disposition—I'm sure in more ways than one. You must be proficient in everything you do."

Her face contorted with anger. Gilda replied with more derogatory insults. Then he put his hand on her throat and began to choke her ever so slightly, but no intentions of death. As he did that, that seemed to calm her down into submission.

He muttered, "Now, is that any way to treat your new friend? Show some respect."

Gilda's grandmother came from the back kitchen concerned and unraveled. VonBrutal used a tone of voice the old woman never heard before which terrified her which was a growing snapping sound, and he said to her he would deal with her later in a dog like voice. What the Grandmother sensed and what Gilda heard were two different things. The woman went back to the kitchen to get a butcher's knife to put in her apron.

At that point, Frans stared Gilda down, grabbed her wrist, and pulled her toward him. He smelled her hair as he forcefully grabbed her long brown mane. He said, "Let's come to an understanding." Then he gave the sweetest smile and kissed her neck. While grabbing her breast he buried his face in her cleavage. The rest of the patrons soon ran out.

She pulled away and punched him in the nose. That seemed to excite VonBrutal even more. He laughed, "that felt like a feather."

He interjected, "Never! Never act that way toward me!"

Gilda added, "Chivalry is dead, you putrid Nazi!" This was as if she had identified what he was too many times. She had gotten redundant.

He grabbed her tight and pulled her in, staring her down with his seductive eyes. "You are now mine. SIT! I'M STILL EATING!" He took his time eating while he watched her. The other customers in the tavern were already gone. No one cared enough to help her. Frans studied her disposition. She was a woman with a complicated mind and an air of demeanor for a greater cause.

Gilda was a cool, calm and collected gal for her age, and she had an abundance of sexuality and beauty. Although she was clever, she was the type of woman men would want to be around continuingly smiling and laughing. Besides, she spoke and read five different languages that she taught herself with her grandmother's aid. A woman's intelligence could be a downfall in a man's world. Frans knew exactly how he was going to use her. He did not ask anything about her life, because that was irrelevant. Women were on earth merely for men's pleasure. Were they not? Of course, they were here for the absolute servitude of men. So, he was to feed on her female emotions to get her to do what he wanted. He would make sure to keep her in a state of confusion.

Frans had his new hostage and slave. Wow, did he ever feel powerful because she has an attachment to him. The way she looked at him was inviting. Her eyes dilated, and her breath changed in his presence. He knew that he could use her to access information from unsuspecting foreigners because men love to tell their secrets to pretty women. He could use her for the sake of just using her with all enjoyment. Altogether, he had a win-win situation. Having someone to control was enticing to him, but that entailed some work. She was to be his servant, concubine, and espionage confidant to extract knowledge from individuals targeted. This was already going as planned, and how easy kidnapping was as a superior and as a Nazi. Frans thought, "What a delightful little dish!" Yet, there was something about her that pulled him in. VonBrutal genially adored her.

The day was going on to evening. As the sun set, the most bizarre shadows danced on the walls of the tavern. The sun seemed to streak and contort defiantly by not welcoming the night. The illusion was that it was holding on to the light, because in darkness, all is fair game. Night came, and the air was still. The two were now alone in the bar. Except for the grandmother clanking around the kitchen. He watched her. He really watched her and grew warm. As he took his hands and rubbed his thighs, his mouth watered.

He felt himself aroused, and knowing she was a barmaid, she would hardly be a virgin. Frans interjected, "Your room is upstairs, is it not?"

Her face was blank. All color washed out. She was not expecting this today, nor any other day. Gilda thought this was just going to be another night serving drinks and wiping tables. His dark hungry look intrigued her, yet she never at the time knew she was losing herself. And, in the end she would be nothing but a tasty morsel to that wolf.

He grabbed her hair and forced her to stand. With his hand on her head and an arm around her back, he stared her down penetratingly and said, "What would you prefer more, my hands wrapped around your neck or my knife pressed on your jugular vein? It's your choice." There was no response from her, but her jaw dropped. Some time passed. In all actuality, it was a lot of time. Her heart pounded in her chest as he pressed himself against her. Then, Frans began to claw at her long red dress and bodice. She felt herself doomed, as a servant to its master.

Grabbing her firmly, Frans dragged her upstairs to a room. As he slammed the door, he threw her down on the bed and said, "You are coming to Sofia with me. And you will be in my service, working for me as I demand. Do you understand what I am saying?"

She nodded.

Nicely he said, "Now take your clothing off!" He watched her as he also undressed. Then VonBrutal seemed to melt, as there was a reflection in his personality that made him warm. He climbed onto the bed, kissing her ever so sweetly with loving caresses. He spread open her thighs as he ran his hands on her back cheeks. By taking his long, boney middle finger, he pushed it in to her anus and began to wiggle it around with provocative intentions. When he lay on top of her, she welled up such a warmth of euphoria as VonBrutal's cock trusted inside of her. Than somehow, he arched around and with his member still inside he curtailed himself and buried his mouth of her left ass cheek.

VonBrutal sucked for a duration. Then with a growing appetite he bit her.

Gilda was in orgasm, so she did not seem to notice right way. When she opened her eyes to focused, Frans appeared to be so hairy like a beast. She seemed to fade in and out of reality. What she was feeling was surreal and she drifted onto a metaphysical plane. Frans got the iron he needed to regain his strength.

Gilda passed out. Frans still hairy like a dog heard some thumping coming from the steps. He knew. Not getting dressed, he stealthily got up and moved without any sound towards his advance of the bedroom door, and through the blacken staircase which he descended. He met grandma on the fifth step and VonBrutal reached into her apron and graded the butcher's knife. Slicing her throat, he did not allow her fall with a thump. He sported her weight and quickly dragged her into the kitchen where he dumped her body. While there he packed provision in a wicker basket for the neck days' journey. Thinking ahead, he placed the basket on a table in the tavern for easy admission in the morning with no questions asked.

Frans as his usually movements entailed mountaineering the steps to the room where Gilda was sleeping. As he was observing her beauty as he thought that she could sleep through Armageddon. With his nakedness he curled up to her back side. Stroking her cheeks, he moved his member into her anus and began the thrust as he gripped her breast. Then he brazed his wolf teeth in to her right side as he was still inside of her penetrating her essence. In between of drinking her blood, he licked her open wound like a puppy. She seemed to be awake but not. Yet, in the morning she never noticed that she was covered with purple bruises.

Frans awakened Gilda in the morning while it was still dark by throwing her red dress at her and yelled, "Get dressed! Now!"

At first, Gilda acted as if she was not awake. VonBrutal had thrown her dress on her face. She grabbed her dress and got dressed. Then she walked over to the corner and vomited. He yelled as he grabbed her red cap out of her closet and through that at her too, "get yourself together."

She was able to compose herself. They descended the steps from her room and entered the tavern. She asked to say goodbye to her Grandmother. With no response, VonBrutal snatched the picnic basket from the table and shoved it into Gilda's arm. He said conservatively as he smiled and winked, "hold this." When he turned his back, she peaked inside the basket, and knew her grandmother did not pack that unorganized mess. Swiftly, he grabbed numerous bottles of liquor.

VonBrutal looked under the bar counter and snitched a

dozen packs of cigarettes. Than with a shove, he pushed

Gilda out the door. She maintained her balance before

falling down the steps. With a hop skip and jump she

landed on the dirt road close to his BMW. She was not

quite sure what she was felling which was something

between fear, fascination and the adventure. She even

smiled for a moment. Than VonBrutal abruptly said as

he already knew, "what are you thinking?" She said,

"nothing." He demanded, "TELL ME!" She thought,

"you are so fucking intrusive." He said, "Watch what

you think young lady. Get on the back of my bike now."

He stuffed the bottles and smokes into the sidecar. "Do

not let your long dress get caught in the wheel and keep

your feet off the exhaust pipes. I do not need any melted

shoes ruining my bike! Do you understand what I am

saying to you? If you chose to fall off the back of the

bike, I AM LEAVING YOUR ASS THERE! And most of all watch what you are thinking!"

Off they went. Gilda clutched her dress and cape while holding the wicker basket. Down the rocky dirt road, they roamed off to Sofia, Bulgaria. The night was fading, and the reluctant Sun resisted to shine its rays. That morning there was a clear division between night and day. The night was almost about to win when at last there was the full light of the day. Yet, the landscape was still kind of creepy. In the early morning hours, the couple passed down through another winding road in which an ancient church had its tower bells chiming. The sound was eerie and disturbed which seemed to linger on with a bizarre echo. VonBrutal muttered with derogatory expressions that this leg of the journey will take over four days lugging her around.

Then, Gilda began to weep like a baby with tears rolling down her face and snot running from her nose. She was sobbing so hard that her chest was heaving and contorting. While he was annoyed, VonBrutal stop his bike and turned around and smiled by saying, "Now there my love. Just relax and enjoy the trip." That seemed to facilitate the calming down of his hostage. He took a handkerchief out of his jacket and he smushed it on her face abruptly wiping the snot and tears from her countenance. VonBrutal added, "come on girl we got to move on." That seemed to shut her up. They continued though the back roads of Romania to Bulgaria. There in Sophia Tötung had given Frans an address for his occupancy.

Chapter 2

*That seemed to shut her up. They continued though the
back roads of Romania to Bulgaria. There in Sophia
Tötung had given Frans an address for his occupancy.*

The four-day trip to Sophia turned into a month-
long adventure.   VonBrutal was confused about his
newly found hostage. He stopped his motorcycle at
various intervals to contend with his property otherwise
known as Gilda. About every hour he pulled over and
talked to her nicely yet still controlling. She got off the
back of the bike to stretch her legs and pee in the bushes.
He developed a fascination with her. Gilda was not a
normal sort of being. When he smiled at her, she seemed
to relax.   Their first night in the frontier was the most
awkward. VonBrutal did not have a bed roll for her. Not
being sure of where she was to sleep, he laid down his
mat and curled up alongside her ass.   As she drifted off

to slumber, he enunciated that she needed to watch her thoughts as he whispered in her ear.

The mornings came as that does every day especially on dark days. The two cruised along with VonBrutal being lost in the woods because he was a "dumbass". Yet, Gilda knew the way since she was from that area. She chose not to say anything for obvious reasons. He stopped at unusually outposts where people gathered, and booze were served. At these drinking establishment, he never bothered to ask for directions to get to the border of Romania. This was a frolic time. The drunken individual did not have to work and could still feel important besides keep composed in a manly disposition. The camping went on for days turning into a month, and Gilda did not say more than three sentences. She could not speak, and why would she have wanted too? VonBrutal left her alone for the short duration being without any harassment.

Nonetheless, there was a sudden down pour. The torrential rains were ominously falling rapidly and in copious quantities. They pulled off to the side of the road with no shelter insight. Gilda stood on the dirt road, and the rain poured over her. The cold spring wetness drenched her as a soaked rat.   The day went into evening, and she was freezing. VonBrutal was pissed because he could not even light a cigarette. Without much reconciliation, he pulled out a bottle of booze and took a couple of deep swigs than pass the bottle to her. VonBrutal enunciated himself clearly, "DRINK! And, keep drinking until you are warmed. Do you understand me?" Gilda did not say a dam thing; she just inhaled the bottle of alcohol. Within seconds, the girl felt a Hell of a lot better. She seemed to undulate for a time in a sensuously smooth disposition. Yet, the senses have the probability of affected the intellect. Gilda ran her hand over top of her head relinquishing the weight of the water on her head even though the rain poured in the most confusing fashion. This was a matter of self-composure to regain part of herself.

VonBrutal pulled his jacket over his head and lite a smoke that was in his inner lining. He smoked as a madman because that was what he did. Still he made conversation, "What was your live like as a child?"

Gilda looked at him as if he was an idiot, and thought, "Why do you want to know?"

He retorted, "if you have not realized at this point that I can read your thoughts and mine yours."

She said, "what is this?"

His response, "in time you will understand."

VonBrutal repeated the same question twice, "What was

your childhood like?"

Affirming her soaking wet inner man, the little

woman took a prolonged point in notice to his inimical

comment. She expressed the question spoken to her, "My

Grandmother raised me. I never knew my parents. She

told me I was with her since I was two years old. My

Grammie raised me well. She taught five different

foreign languages and about the world. I was well feed,

and always warm. As a young child she read bedtime

storied to me about fairytales. One that was so repeated

was a picture story of young maidens who had to cater to

trolls by rubbing and scratching their grime heads. When

the maidens did so, gold would fall from their long locks

as they brushed their hair. When the maidens refused to

take care of the trolls, frogs would jump from their mouths. Grammie read this story many times.

VonBrutal chuckled profusely, "it pays to be nice to men."

Within moments, they heard a car coming down the road in the early morning light, but it was not quite morning anymore. The rain still did not let up. There was a mist in the air, and strange birds were squawking in the distance. The abrupt noise of the car came closer. A 1930 Maybach Zeppelin 12-cylinder DS pulled up. The paint was chipped, and there was an abundancy of rust. A voice cried out, "hey, fuckhead. It's Fledermaus." Gilda thought, "his name is Bat in German. How strange."

Fledermaus yelled again, "Get the girl in the car, and your motorcycle back on the road. The Sun is coming up fast which might actually happen in this neck of the woods. We are only a couple of miles from my homestead. I have been hearing your whining thoughts for hours. You are a fucking idiot. Could you not have known that you were only in walking distance from my villa? Why are you the Reich's most gifted agent? fucking unbelievable!"

Fledermaus said all the of harassing statement to VonBrutal with a delightful grin on his face. He was a tall lanky man with long frizzy orange hair. He always wore a top hat and aviator glasses even at night. He was a real shaggy sort of guy. With no regards for current events, Fledermaus had a laid-back disposition even though there was a seriousness pertaining to the work at hand which was his own pleasure.

VonBrutal said, "brother it is good to see you." VonBrutal was merely taken back for a moment by the derogatory guy language.

Fledermaus had a cigarette handing from his mouth with an inch of ashes ready to fall off. He said, "if the lady wants to get warm and have a smoke, she has to get her beautiful ass into my car. What's going on VonBrutal? Can't you get your BMW out of the fucking mud? Let's get a move on. I got to get some sleep!"

Gilda stopped hesitating and hopped into the rusty yellow Maybach. She got her red cap caught in the door. Fledermaus said, "lovely lady compose yourself. Please."

So, she did. Fledermaus pulled forward, but only for a half mile. Nevertheless, he started smelling and kissing her hand. She permeated a delightful fragrance which made his mouth water. At this point she was getting tired especially because he had the heat on. Her eyes were closed and sitting in a car was nice. Than Fledermaus began to caress her forearm with sweet caresses. He focused on the crease behind her elbow.

That's where he sunk his teeth into her forearm, and she did not even know it because she was half asleep. For Fledermaus that was a bed time snack, yet her essence was quite tasty. Quickly following, he returned to his homestead which was a rickety wooden one level with a sprawling subterrestrial chambers. Upon arriving, he immediately went in leaving Gilda in the car sleeping. He took a beeline for the basement and crashed like something fierce and barbaric into a deep slumber on his king-size bed with his blanket over his head. His underground establishment was surrounded with Picasso paintings. He loved the "artcy-fartcy" community of Europe and was a proud supporter at night. The basement had all the same accommodations as the above level of the homestead. Fledermaus LOVED to have guests and make them feel comfortable as much as he could. There he slept in comfort for the duration of the day as the region's best kept secret.

After some time, VonBrutal finally got his bike out of the mud, and was out to find Gilda. All this duration, he was hearing music in his head from the Devil. He was becoming aggravated that Fledermaus took off with his girl as an abrupt symphony. His jovial buddy abandoned him without lending comradery and Fledermaus laughed at him. As the weight of non-respect fell upon VonBrutal he thought, "that bastard!" VonBrutal also knew what an opportunist Fledermaus was, and how he could sweet talk the ladies. Most of all, Fledermaus was the best liar when the issue was of his personal wants or selfishness. He was a strange sort of guy as was VonBrutal. A people person was Fledermaus' nature who loved people and the distant country roads they traveled to pick them up as victims. His homestead in Romania was one of his better options because his property was centrally located in the woods near by serval towns in each direction. Fledermaus found both male and female companionship with ease. Yet, most of his newly found friends were not alive in the morning. Too bad for them. Unless, he struck up a special kindship with some of them for future endeavors. He was a drug addict. His drug was A+ which was the tastiest because that blood was salty and sweet simultaneously which lingered on his palate for the duration. Females were always the easiest to connive because they were looking for something else. Sometimes Fledermaus fairer victims wanted sex or were seeking out love. The reality was that they knew he had money, and the girls just wanted some "fucking help or relief." The males he disposed of desired comfort and acceptance of their homosexuality. Fledermaus knew people and their thoughts. Either wise, he had the upper hand and reveled in it by filling his belly up with their blood. One hundred feet from Fledermaus playing field was a deep long ditch dug for body dumpage. The rolling stench was far enough from his home, and the pit was surrounded by a lavender field on all sides which strangely enough in every season was in blossom.

People forget in time which overpowers individual's distant recollections. Fledermaus had an unusual romance with the locals. More description about this bullshit was that he was liked but he killed his friends, and everyone associated with them. People knew about him and dreaded, and for whatever reason welcomed him. Fledermaus did not even know how old he was anymore by 1939. His memories were nothing but darkness in a party atmosphere and a strange sort of lovemaking. He even had old clothing dating back over the last couple of hundreds of years. Loneliness was never an issue. There was a bounty of human beings for playtime. Besides, he had other weird friends such as the gang of Nazi bikers.

Abruptly, a prolonged banging commenced on Fledermaus' door. VonBrutal was infuriated and yelled numerous derogatory statements. This went on for some time, and Fledermaus finally remembered to get up and unlock the door. Fledermaus merely smiled, and said to VonBrutal, "come in and if you did not realize your girl is sleeping in the car like a baby. Make yourselves at home and light a fire if you please. Now, I am going back to bed, and will be up at dusk. By the way we will be expecting other associates later this evening. So, do not disturb me anymore. Ta-ta."

VonBrutal also being a selfish bastard took a quick survey of Fledermaus' residency. There were all the accommodations of home and food in the ice box. The pantry was stocked which was enough to feed an army. Certainly, the nocturnal gentleman had an assortment of elegant spices. Otherwise, the place was clean except for one bedroom. Knowing that Fledermaus was a lazy individual, there must be a caretaker living on the grounds.

The morning mist rested on the ground. VonBrutal yelled for Gilda as he was calling for a dog as he stormed out of the house. The yellow car was parked by the garage. For a split moment, the caretaker peeked out through the window, and decide to leave that situation at hand.

Gilda never heard the disruption. She was exhausted besides a prisoner. VonBrutal marched over with anticipation. He was relieved that she was still there. He jerked open the door, and she fell out onto the rocky muddy ground. Bewildered, Gilda opened her eyes, and disillusioned by thinking "what now." He yelled at her, "stop thinking. There is going to be so much 'what now' for the continuance of your life." He picked the girl up and put her on her feet, and said, "look my lady we are going to go in and get some rest."

Composing herself, she had no choice because there was nowhere else to go. Gilda was hungry and tired which was irrelevant. They got into Fledermaus house and VonBrutal told her to go to bed. She thought, "where?" he yelled back, "just go to bed!" She gritted her teeth and walked to the back of the house to an old room where there was a layer of dust on the bedcover that had not been slept in for some years which was the only dirty room in the house. The wheels in her head were beginning to turn by not utilizing readily detectible underlining thoughts. Some thoughts were from a refined mind and were as gentle complex notes which is the opposite of a Polly Anna deposition trying to make everything positive. Nothing in the world must be ok with numerous possible outcomes as some delusional subconscious disposition. There were variables. There were many variables.

The day passed, and evening presented itself as a beautiful beast. Fledermaus began to stir in his underground wing of his home by mumbling, "oh fuck and oh fuck some more!" VonBrutal passed out in the living room because he was still tired. Gilda woke up feeling trapped because she was. There was some stirring outside as the groundskeeper scrambled around. The noise brought the house to consciousness. The rumbling of pipes reverberated off the windows as twenty motorcycles convened onto Fledermaus homestead. The commotion was enough to wake up the dead in the lavender field. The caretaker hated when the pack rolled in. He cringed and shook his fist.

The Nazi bikers dismounted from their money run of robbing rich Jews of gold, diamonds and bonds besides information gathered though various ways. Also, there were given the responsibility to ensure Nazi strategic agendas because to the geographic position of their tour of Eastern Europe and especially Bulgaria that neighbored with Turkey on the Black Sea besides the Aegean Sea. They were too influence Bulgarian politic to keep the country under the Axis agenda. Threats, violence and abrupt conversation were easy tactics to utilize.

Upon arrival the men were fatigued. Most of them did not walk far to take a leek. Monte pissed on Fledermaus' Maybach which made some profound streaks and let out an evil laugh as he relieved himself. Three of their riders picked up girls along the ride from Berlin for entertainment and to share with the other men. Destiny, Alexus and Cadim were feeling pretty and important to go along for the destination. Also, Tötung met up with the pack along the road, and he was there for the evening wanting to observe Gilda's beauty.

Destiny, Alexus and Cadim watched Monte as he relieved himself, and the girls were almost standing at attention and ecstatic to observe that man took a piss. Of course, Monte was a wild man, yet he had reserved and stoic attributes. He was a strong man and a pack master in the same ranking as Tötung with wisdom and supreme logical thinking. He was very much up there, yet super sexy. Monte was the younger and a chic magnet and decide to have the girls before they were diner. With one glance of the eye he beckoned them over to the other side of the Maybach by thrusting one and yelling at the other two to raise their skirts in a supersonic sexual frenzy. His cock was feeling fine as he walked away from the dismayed women because he was fast and proficient. Monte could have taken his time, but he had business to attend too. Women loved him, and men respected him. He was protective of his bothers even though VonBrutal was a thorn in his side. Monte resented him because VonBrutal was spoiled, and always got everything for the fact VonBrutal was from money. Monte grew up having to eat chicken-bone soup. He thought, "that bastard."

VonBrutal popped out of the front door of the homestead and said, "brother it is good to see you." He strolled over to Monte. VonBrutal gave him a bear hug. Then he realized that Tötung was there, and shared greetings with the older gentleman biker. Monte reverberated the exchange, and got a digging comment to VonBrutal, "why don't you just be simple?"

VonBrutal looked at Monte because of his derogatory comment as the filter in his brain did not even allow that concept in. VonBrutal said repeatedly, "brothers. All of you. It is so good to see you."

The caretaker was stressed with putting on the diner party. He was trying to hull the 20-gallon cast-iron kettle from the barn along with the supporting apparatuses for the pot by dragging it along the ground which made tracks in the dirt. Then there was the stack of wood and kindling that the caretaker had to arrange. Where was he to find the fire starter? Then the boys started shooting their guns in the old man's direction for playful amusement. On that cool evening, the caretaker was sweating profusely. This was the last thing he wanted to do that moment. The caretaker thought, "that Nazi biker scum!"

Fledermaus came out the front door to the homestead yawning and stretching his arms in his lazy demeanor. His frizzy orange hair was in every direction. Then he recalled putting on his top hap. He said, "now, now will someone help my old caretaker. We have a diner party to put on with many conversations to conduct and women to consume."

The pack master Monte gave a glace, and the work was done for the old caretaker. There was help bringing out the 50 pounds of marinated beef for the sauerbraten that was flavored in Riesling from the Rhineland for more than three days with half a container of Turkish Bay Leaf and the finest rosemary vinegar from a monastery in Avignon, France. The caretaker was becoming feeble cutting up the onions and celery on a propped-up board by the kettle. VonBrutal yelled for Gilda. Monte interjected, "Destiny cut the veggies NOW!" There was a huge burlap bag by the board. She rolled her eyes and commenced which took her about an hour. She had to keep fixing her hair. In the meantime, a container of black peppercorn was added into the boiling water of the kettle along with salt and two pounds bacon fat. Fledermaus graciously said to the caretaker as he licked his lips, "oh please do not forget the berbere spice because flavor is all good and keep stirring the pot."

Time had passed, and VonBrutal was becoming perturbed with his hostage. He stormed around in circles. The other men looked at him as if he was an idiot. Once again, he yelled, "Gilda!"

Tötung as the refined gentleman that he was said in a deep, cool, calm and collect voice, "VonBrutal sit down and have some sort of German beverage. I will go in and find the girl the lovely thing that she is." Tötung strolled away from veranda, the warmth of the fire and the smell of roasting beef to find Gilda. He took his time smelling the air, and he detected fear which was a warming sensation for him. Gilda was standing inside by the door when Tötung entered. He said, "my-my... aren't you a tasty treat. Let me look at you. Now please turn around and lift your dress. He regarded her as he ran his hand on her backside. That was perfection." Some moments passed, and his hand was still caressing her ass cheeks. He ran his finger between her buttocks to feel her warm moist pussy then said, "how beautiful is that." Then Tötung kissed her on the check and escorted her out to the veranda as she pulled her dress down.

The outdoor night part was on the way. Tables and chairs were taken out of the barn and set up for the Nazi bikers. The musician finally showed up. They walked miles to get to Fledermaus' homestead. There was a flute, oboe and a tribal drummer. The music was arranged to German passé décor, yet quiet moving and delightful. The uplifted Fledermaus always put on the best diner parties. The sweet melody was moved by the inspiration of the beat and inspirational. The evening was on the way. And, the man named Fledermaus translated to Bat was quite elated, and especially delighted with his company. His disposition was obvious because the night crawler clapped his hands frequently. He smiled when the biker recommenced at shooting off guns to terrorize his old caretaker. All of them were pointing their weapons towards the caretaker making the old man jump. That was just for entertainment. They never intended on hitting him. Monte aimed near enough to graze his clothing. The caretaker turned around and gave Monte a dirty look. He said, "lighten up old man this is all genuine libation." The caretaker retreated to his apartment above the garage because his work was done and traumatized as usually.

Gilda made her appearance on the sight. The girls, Dynasty, Alexus and Cadim were pissed to see the Transylvanian beauty. They laughed like something fierce because Gilda wore a long red cap that was so outdated. The female aggression was on the way with their brutal facial expressions which was beyond standard nonverbal communication. Yet, the three girls were exhibiting the sound of hissing snakes as they spoke of Gilda. The female concubines were pissed that Gilda was the favored guest and had more sex appeal that all three of them combined, and the girls found ways to harass Gilda. The girls scorn was commencing concurrently with chants of "Hail Hitler" among the bikers. The "ride-alongs" all giggled as the men announced, "let's see what kind of profit we can turn especially Eastern Europe. Ha. ha...ha."

Indian a lead rider came forth and elaborated his knowledge, "we have South America and Africa at our disposable." He said this as he shot his gun into the air as he grabbed his balls by shouting derogatory comments.

"We are going to make so much money with taking over the world!"

Indian was the most road worn and muddy from the ride. He had his old lady back in Berlin that was kept under control. Yet, he was rarely home. The lifestyle of being in various locations was interesting by emerging himself in the Reich's endeavors was his main calling besides he identified himself with the likeminded men. Indian was the serjeant of the arms of the pack which is the rule enforcer and rule maker when necessary. What else could be said about this guy because he was highly intelligent in a medieval sort of fashion. He was a tall man of 6'2" with a cock that fit the proportions of a big man. That night his hair was long and stringy. He was riding in front of the as lead riddled with mud especially in his hair. His shoulders hurt from holding the handlebars. Thus, upon arrival at the homestead he was tired, and not in the mood to be bothered by any trivial nonsense. Being tired made him feel resentful. He was heavily endowed in the Nazi network by being modest yet proud. That night he was eyeballing Destiny even though she did not have big tits to his licking. There were not any other options that evening. Sometimes a man had to lower his standers for consortium. He often had sex with the female sort that he found repulsive so to ease his manliness. Indian did not like having to drag his property down to Romania. He would have preferred to leave his property back in Berlin. She was acting up again. The girl kept clanking around with the bracelets on her wrists which he found annoying. Indian thought, "that ungrateful bitch!"

Indian had moxie. He did security at Hitler's beer hall putsch and even at the night at the Bürgerbraukeller the pinnacle of the Nazi movement in 1923 as the young energetic man that he was full of motivation and stout beer. Setting fire to the Reichstag in 1933 was also of his doing after a long night of drinking. A side door was broken into where upon Indian and some other boys brought in supplies to burn the place down.

There was a break in consciousness. Then Monte belched out, "shut the fuck up you lame old fucking bat." He got sick of swallowing his pride and having to defer to other stupid fucking men that were innately inferior to him. At that change, there was still so much disgruntle behavior. A voice rang out, "we have more work to do in the name of order!" At that point things seem to explode. The drinking had progressed too far.

Indian was up in arms, "look at everything I have done. I was a moving catalyst."

Then Fledermaus had to laugh by saying, "What! What! Lookie-lookie at everything I have done. Ha he."

Indian's rage was boiling as Fledermaus' musicians played the love story song and strung their instruments to beautiful notes. The chiming and intriguing melody coincided with all Hell breaking loss. Indian got up and slammed his spiked helmet into Destiny's right temple. The man got done using her as a prostitute for gathering intelligence information among the German elite. He used her at social galas to flop on her back. At some point, Indian just thought of Destiny as a disrespectful "cunt." As he did the act, he recalled how he crucified her to a tree in the back yard and left her there all day with nails in her wrists and feet only because she was not being a good worker.

A reiteration fell upon the obscure violence. Fledermaus said boys lets relax and just eat the girls who are in ear reach hearing us. Would that not be grand? Let's do it!" Alexus and Cadim ran into the woods screaming as bullets flew. Then music never stopped as elegant as the notes were contrasting the abject terror resignation from the young women. Gilda stood close to the fire in a blackout.

Fledermaus elegant voice range out, "would you boys be so kind as to throw the bodies into the ditch in the lavender field. Now, I am going inside to rest." With all laziness he went inside.

At that point, the party was winding down and the musician left. Most of the men went into for slumber. The fire was nothing but ambers. The leftover sauerbraten was left in the cauldron. The mess was work for the old caretaker to contend with. Scavenger birds squawked as the night slowly dissipated. Gilda stood there frozen, blank and unresponsive. Tötung said to VonBrutal, "now you do still have the key and location of the flat in Sophia?" VonBrutal hesitated. Tötung said, "you fucking idiot! Now, go through your stuff and find it!" Without delay, he did so by pulling everything out of his sidecar until he resolved his stupidity. Tötung commanded to VonBrutal, "pick the girl up and put her in the sidecar. Tuck your blankets around her. She is a precious commodity. Get a move on!"

VonBrutal and Gilda got back on the road to Sophia. She was slumped over as they road down the dirt rocky road. The ride only lasted for a day and was uneventful. Upon arrival, he set up shop. Months passed, and winter fell.

Chapter Three

The evening settled in on a winter's night in 1940. The air was frigid, and the times were dark. James Benson moved along the crowded streets of Sofia, clutching his designer attaché case. He had been sent on a special mission by President Roosevelt to secure certain assets, possessions, properties, and liaisons within the Eastern European states. The Balkans, besides being a wheat producer, were rich in coal, iron ore, petroleum, natural gas, and bauxite which was a clayey rock used to produce aluminum. The hope was that these resources could counterbalance the German Nazis. Even though this was a feeble venture, he was going forward just the same. This was an attempt not to lose all, and even how difficult it was not to have the upper hand.

At that time, Bulgaria was still neutral in the war, and the Americans were not yet fully engaged. Bulgaria was a jackpot for to gain since it opened to the Black Sea, and the country maintained an allure for spies. What else were they to do but to be spies under any circumstances? Times were precarious, because the world had ceased to spin on its axis, and all hell had broken out across the world. The insanity of utter darkness spouted its wave of abject terror. No one spoke about the horrifying reality. No one wanted to acknowledge what was transpiring in Europe. They were only peeking at what was happening, yet they knew as a slideshow was progressing.

Feeling the cold seeping through his overcoat, James was happy to get to his next location, where he would meet his old buddy Hans, a Hungarian spy whom he'd known for years who was otherwise known as Indian. Pulling his silver case of cigarettes from his overcoat, James lit one up; he could barely see the smoke rise under the awning of a storefront. Smoking it down to the butt, he tossed the remnant into the street. Quickly, he descended a flight of stairs to get to the entrance of La Boîte de Nuit des Filles Dansantes, where an usher opened the door and welcomed him into the large club. The French-fashioned nightclub had a subtle and accepting social ambiance; a band was playing, and smoke was streaming throughout the room.

Leaning forward by crossing her arms to enhance her cleavage, the coat-check girl asked for James's coat and hat. As she smiled, she used her persuasion while insisting on him giving her his attaché case. He clutched the leather-bound designer bag and politely said, "no." James moved to the bar, making his way through a crowded room with a smorgasbord of people of different nationalities and dispositions. He waited and ordered a

Kentucky whiskey with soda water. Drinking it with enjoyment, he felt himself transforming as the alcohol warmed him. The beverage went down easily and put him into a peaceful euphoria. James looked around. No sign of Hans. So, he ordered another whiskey on an empty stomach. Turning at an angle, he leaned upon the bar with his elbow propped so he could see the band playing. Pulling a scrap of paper out of his pocket, he reviewed his notes from earlier that day. On his notepad, he scribbled the barbed wire of a killing center with the Nazi swastika on it. Rumor had it that they were planning to gas the Jews, and they had made the preparations years earlier by gathering the chemicals and resources to do so, knowing full well that the United States was not going to do anything to deter the liquidation of millions of human beings. That knowledge was prevalent prior to Hitler's speech of the Final Solution.

His focus shifted to the music and ambiance. The environment was gay and entertaining. James reflected back as he was pulled into reality to the day at hand. Yet, he knew the information gathered would be to no avail. The point was that the American government could not care less about the genocide or anyone else who got caught up in that storm.

The atmosphere of the nightclub was delightful. The lighting was perfect, and the decor was inviting. La Boîte de Nuit des Filles was the most popular nightclub in Sofia for men. There were many people drinking immense amounts of alcohol and many being served dinner of the most extravagant cuisine. Then the announcer, who was dressed in tux and tails, declared that the main entertainment would begin soon. Not long after this, Hans put his hand on James's back and said, "I am glad you found the joint all right. Let's get a table.

The food is unbelievable, and the women are soft. The girls are so friendly. You'll see."

The two debonair gentlemen were escorted to a table in a prime location in front of the stage. The band recommenced, and then a dozen girls came out from various directions, scantily dressed in satin costumes. They wore very short skirts that barely covered their derrieres, along with bare midriffs and low-cut tops that showed way too much cleavage. The dancers had the high energy necessary for this entertainment. They were young—not much older than nineteen each. The excitement in the room was building. James's expression even enhanced how attractive he was, with his jet-black hair, dark piercing eyes, and debonair smile. He found himself having a rather enjoyable time in Bulgaria, of all places. The drinks came at some point, and the two forgot about ordering dinner until it was just about time for the kitchen to close. The evening wore on.

One of the girls intrigued him. She radiated glee as she pranced about. James had never seen more beautiful legs, complemented with the most perfect ass. The Romanian dancing girl was quite delightful, and her long hair seemed to be alive with anticipation of him running his fingers through it. He was quite taken back, and he found himself fascinated, saying to himself, "She is someone special, and I would like to get to know her."

When he mentioned to Hans her heartbreaking beauty, Hans interjected, "Would you like to meet her? A perfect ass is something to fall in love with."

James replied, "But she's a prostitute."

Hans said, "Dancers are people too. That is how they make their money."

The night progressed as the music became more enjoyable; a few more drinks later and James did not seem to care. Observing her beauty, he became entranced. At that moment, nothing seemed to matter. He was even more impressed by her moxie. She was looking good, really good, when Hans called her over, and in front of them she moved in every single seductive way a woman could in order to get attention from a man. James was quite stunned when   asked out loud what he thought, "Would you like to make love?"

Gilda's response was, "Oh." She thought, "I have a boyfriend who's a Nazi operative with whom I have a relationship." James heard that and responded, "that does not matter."

So that was what she thought at the time. She had some false ideology that bonded her to that guy. Her boyfriend was just using her, as men do, for his own selfish interests.

Gilda said to James as she leaned forward, revealing her delicious cleavage and smiling like Aphrodite herself, as the ultimate temptress who was any man's dream, "Let's have some drinks."

James thought, "Why not? What can go wrong with drinking with a beautiful woman?" The beverages came in numerous rounds. And at some point, she knew that he knew that she knew that he knew she was strictly turning a profit. The mutual understanding came into play. She felt fine because all her drinks were colored water. The drink commission was lucrative until the customer figured out the faux pas. Why not? A girl got to make a living. Young beautiful women need to be paid for their companionship, or at least some sort of compensation. Love is randomly the case yet always welcomed in great multitudes.

The young sex goddess who was exclusively valued for her persuasion excused herself for a moment. She went down the steps to the dressing room to change. Dropping her satiny costume on the floor, she hunted around the dressing room which she shared with all the other girls for her dress. Cloaking herself, she then pulled up her stockings and fit them into place. Tightening her corset, Gilda used it to push her boobs together so that they bulged out of her dress. The woman could not help how beautiful she was. Looking at herself in the mirror, she realized, "Damn, I look great! I want James to fall in love with how soft my skin is. I know he is not going to be in my life for long, but James is the motivation for me getting out of this troubled relationship and maybe moving on with my life. I feel that I have known him forever, and I know that this is only a brief encounter. I shouldn't say no. I feel as if I had dreamed about him in some past and in some distant fairy-tale nonsense romance."

Yet, then again, fairy tales were always stories, or were they lies? The realist would say that love at first sight was only for idiots and retards. A person with a gentler, calmer persuasion would say yes to a once-in-a-lifetime romance. This was the passion and hope or was this the love that could light up a difficult life's existence and then turn to emptiness. She was to be worse off in the end.

Planted there was a note tucked into her coat from Mr. Nazi. She read it and tossed it into her pocket, as she had many times before. He wanted her to steal James's briefcase. VonBrutal was tipped off and spent the night in the nightclub spying on them, and he knew that the briefcase was of the utmost importance to American interests in the Balkans. VonBrutal needed to have the attaché case without fail. Within its documents there would be enough information to set him up with the Nazi party back in Berlin. Thus, the endeavor would make his motorcycle extravaganza even more profound. VonBrutal was proud, as if he had finally arrived at the pinnacle of life.

Radiant she was when she went back to James. She walked out of the dressing room confident and of course dressed. Hans had excused himself to seek his own female companionship. He liked a heavier girl whose boobs were huge. Once he'd found his fascination, Hans would drink the night away with his newfound friend and her voluminous breasts.

Gilda said to James, "Let's get out of here and go to a real party."

He replied, "No, I want to get to know you."
James once again asked, "Do you want to make love?"

Gilda felt his intense passion and melted like a marshmallow over an open flame. The girl got as elated as a perfectly roasted marshmallow could be before it got devoured. This was her first real date ever in her life, even though she was working. The reality was that the Romanian dancing girl was nothing but a sex slave to be used by her male counterparts. To her own misfortune, she fell in love and lost herself in James. The delusions were about herself, because she could have walked away at any point along the road and given up much sadness and despair by participating in a peaceful existence, but there was a war going on. That was what this woman's purpose was: nothing but to serve men's pleasures for other men's profit, especially when it pertained to espionage. That was always the marker in future sneaky endeavors.

She crumpled up the note some more in her pocket. She pulled it out and looked at it. Nervous and bewildered she was as the couple left. Gilda kept thinking about the note.

James pulled her in and whispered as if she heard nothing at all. In all actuality, the whisper sounded like a telepathic moan that gave the profound impact of unspoken significance. They had known each other in a prior life. Now, their meeting was to be brief. The two were to be separated between oceans, war, and time itself as that nonsense usually went. Even though Gilda was being used, she still fell in love with a gentleman. For some short duration of time, she was happy which was a couple of hours.

Something that transpired around James was a magic and mood-setting ambience that pulled people in by making them feel welcomed, loved, and respected. When he walked into a room, the crowds parted and paid him homage, unlike other men. James was a human being who held great presence and esteem, coupled with superb and breathtaking admiration. In other words, he had a presence. This was the individual factor to the utmost entity or particularly a demigod. The most pristine pool could have been described that was an oasis of Aphrodite in comparison to the depth of this man.

They gathered their coats and climbed the steps out to the bustling street. Escorting her, he extended an arm, which was accompanied by sweet caresses. On the streets of Sofia, people took notice of the two as they ascended from the nightclub. Gilda was dressed rather shabbily, and James was dressed to the nines, impeccably styled, as was his confidential briefcase.

He asked the same question repeatedly: "Would you make love to me?"

She finally said, "Yes."

Gilda was drawn in by the most passionate kiss and beautiful embrace, and she lost herself in his intensity. In turn, he knew Gilda was of a different realm. Maybe that was the mysterious Romanian in her, or maybe it was that she had loved him since time in all consciousness had started. Yet, that night, she was just the Romanian dancing girl. At that point, James was not ready to accept that this was something out of the ordinary. This trip was just supposed to be some Nazi pre–World War II mission prior to the United States' entry into that sloppy mess. Falling in love was unthinkable, especially when he had no way to care for

and protect her, with ultimately no resources—or maybe
he never really cared. James knew he would be
abandoning her to fend for herself for many years to
come, which did not bother him in the least. The
appearance was of two people who had known each other
for years. This was no ordinary one-night stand. A
connection was made. James kept looking at his watch.

The two arrived at the entrance of the Hotel
Intercontinental. She thought she should just walk away.
When she turned to do so, he went after her. They went in
and climbed the steps to his room. He let her go first to
watch the sway of her hips. Gilda smiled the whole time.
It was that awkward first encounter when a new couple
just stands in the room before any clothing is removed.
He broke out the bottle of champagne and the two glasses
he'd nabbed. Pleasantly surprised, she drank the first

glass rather quickly. He filled the second glass and she felt the warm euphoria from the champagne. She was not paying attention when the and third was poured, and she finished the bottle.

James interjected, "That was the first alcohol you had tonight. The drinks at the club were colored water." He pulled out the note from her coat pocket and said, "Really? Do you want to do that? What got you mixed up with them?"

At that moment, she used all of her sex appeal to get out of that uncomfortable moment. She loosened her dress and tossed her hair about.

Gilda said, "This is the world I live in. The only opportunities I have are collaborating with such an element. What else am I to do?"

That was enough talk for them, and human nature took over. He pulled her in tight, and she became lost in him. It was as if he even took part of her soul. James loved her intensely that night. The ground began to tremble. Mountains rose from the sea. There were tsunami warnings from coast to coast. There were even little sparkles flying through the air. The encounter was not bad as an Earth moving experience. Then he cuddled profoundly while he slept. Of course, he kept one eye open during the night, because she had been told to get the directives from his briefcase which had been personally assigned to him by President Roosevelt. They pertained to various points in the Balkans and who were to be his contact people. His mission had to be fail-safe. He was one of the best. His attaché case also had a trick compartment where the real directives were stashed. In the morning, she was standing over his case, quite naked. James stared at her ass while she rooted through his bag.

James said, "Really? You got to be kidding me." He got up and pulled out the folder of irrelevant information that was a decoy he had prepared before going to Europe on his mission. He handed it to her. "Give that to them, or whatever that beast is who is using you! You are off the hook, and you'll have something to go back to him with." She was not all that good at being sneaky, because that takes practice.

"Come back to bed." She did until the morning sun was shining through the window.

Chapter Four

The room was filled with brown Einfachbier bottles. The bottles littered the floor in crazy abundance. The Einfachbier bottles were everywhere, especially the bedroom. The piles accumulated in every corner, and there were even bottles on the mounds of dirty laundry. The counters were covered with sprawling beer bottles. There was a mass in all corners. Beer bottles were even littered about the bathroom, with some in the bathtub. The accumulation of months of hard drinking of a demented dark soul. Frans VonBrutal's flat was a dump, yet he walked out each morning with his black Nazi uniform well pressed to perfection, along with a crisp swastika armband. VonBrutal was strange for living like that, because he came from money—a very prominent family in Berlin. This was odd given German values and orderliness. With his father's influence, he easily slipped into the role of a Gestapo agent. His evil side took hold, and alcohol was his best confidant, which took him to an intense mental state of mind. He felt more cleaver, and killing was more enjoyable to him, while inebriated. Bizarre as it was, he had a warm side that could pull a person in, but then his dark nature always dominated. He always felt the devil's presence. Soon his destiny was to rot in hell with the rest of his Nazi buddies.

VonBrutal loved his work and the comradery of his friends. He felt the power in every cell of his being. Nothing gave him more pleasure than to kidnap fleeing Jews who'd taken off from the Reich and hauling them back to Germany for torture and interrogation. He especially liked the torture. Sometimes his victims did not make it that far, because they ended up getting a bullet to the base of their skulls. He loved it. He loved it all. Consequently, at times he saw shadows and strange enigmas that haunted him. He knew he was damned, and he enjoyed every moment of his existence.

VonBrutal thought to himself, "What am I going to do about that girl? She never came back last night with that American's briefcase. That fucking bitch!"

The Sun was rising, and morning was dissipating into midday. Frans felt even more defied as the day wore on. His anger stirred as he threw his Einfachbier bottle across the room. Stepping through his rubbish, VonBrutal left his flat and headed out for some nourishment. In route to the nearest pub, he came in contact with Herr Arnold whose code name was Monte, and VonBrutal nearly barked like a dog, "My ward has gone missing."

Herr Arnold replied, "Are you really that dependent on that young woman, or are you insanely jealous that she was lying with another man last night, as you instructed her to do?"

VonBrutal grunted in anger, and the two proceeded to a location for a late lunch.

Gilda was hot; she was hot with anticipation. She was the toast of the town, and with the attention they paid to her, many gentlemen divulged their secrets, which she obediently relayed to VonBrutal. What they liked about her the most was her ass; in all actuality they fell in love with it. The rumpus was perfect, and any man would say anything to impress her about their clandestine work to get near the type of woman whom they saw as completely acceptable. Amazingly, she was always stunned about what topics her pursuers engaged in. The conversation was unbelievable the amount of information that was handed to her. Yet, Gilda withheld 90 percent of any and all conversations from VonBrutal. Her loyalty was not to that bastard, even though he was good in bed. As much as possible, she played the stupid female role as if she were some sort of provocative idiot. Men always fell for that routine. Gilda was always aware of what was transpiring. Besides, she was that of burning cinders and flames. Women are only valued for their youth and beauty.

VonBrutal was infuriated that Gilda had failed to get the briefcase from James. Gilda conclusively got tired of avoiding him. She thought to herself, "What am I going to do? Is he going to fall for the fake documents?" There was nowhere to go, and she had no other options. Going to face him was abject terror. She found him, or he found her, walking by while he was in the pub with Arnold.

He said as she walked in the door, "There's that little cunt."

The realization came to her suddenly that James had used her for her companionship. She was now in this precarious situation, and James was nowhere in sight. She felt an emotional attachment to a man who was of no help, protection, or assistance. Feeling used and discarded was an upsetting emotion. Besides, now she was in imminent danger. And she thought, "Why did I sleep with him in the first place? For what, so I could be in even more danger? Men always take more than they give. James is probably a married man, and on his way back to the States."

Gilda clenched her teeth and crossed her arms in front of her as if she were holding herself. She stared at them blankly, and her face turned pale white. The absence of color made her look even more guilty. Facing this problem by herself, she could not think of how to remedy the situation. James was long gone, and of course completely and utterly useless to her dilemma. He was just passing through, and he never cared in the first place, because he was a rolling stone and on his own mission. Her predicament had become precarious. She had been abandoned, and she never mattered in the first place.

VonBrutal guzzled the last of his beer. Slamming the mug down on the counter and breaking it, he came toward the girl, grabbing her by the arm and pulling her outside with a forceful toss against the brick wall, whereupon he wrapped his hand around her neck. Profusely, he glared at her.

She let out a whimper and engaged his eyes. He never noticed that she was not crying. Gilda just looked at him and walked away once she freed herself from his grip. He watched her go for about ten paces. Then he came after her with a vengeance. He needed to be in control above all. Frans grabbed her roughly. Looking him in the eye, she was frozen. In the process, she felt for his gun. She leaned in and pulled the trigger on the Kongsberg Colt that was still in his holster and shot. She was keeping hold of the gun when he dropped to the ground with a loud thump.

Gilda imagined that VonBrutal was nothing but a bloody mess because she was so close to the point of contact. VonBrutal said, "you missed…you stupid fucking bitch!" She was neither relieved nor disappointed. Gilda was embarrassed.

Monte known to VonBrutal and Gilda was working with many Allies in Eastern Europe by going with his real name Arnold. He said, "let's all relax, and come inside. We have done some good work here. Our next move is that this little girl heads South and gets a suntan. I am in good cohorts with the American boys. They actually think that Gilda has turned on us."

Not much was said. A change of scenery was to transpire.

That night Gilda caught a Pan Am flight to Mexico City.

Chapter 5

Many people who could leave Europe during the war with the Nazis did so and migrated to Central and South America to begin new lives. The poor or the stubborn who did not leave gave up their property and lost everything when they stayed to face the consequences. Within the masses, there was an influx of private people and refugees who were involved in espionage. This could be described as an interconnected network of underground elements. There was the utmost importance that information was gathered from them, either aiding one side or another. Loyalty was a mixed emotion. The US War Department took notice of these people and utilized them to the max. Those who emigrated from Europe did not have to blend in by having a strong knowledge of Latin American affairs in order to be useful, unlike the American spies who were sent by G-2 Army intelligence, who needed experience living in South and Central America.

Those who had money got the hell out of Europe, especially from the Eastern European states. They were people with the foresight to know that they were doomed under the rising dangerous tide of fascism. The poor were left to the wrath of the Nazis and the Soviet communists. Many sought refuge in various countries from Mexico to the southern tip of Chile. Montevideo, Uruguay, was another hot spot to choose from. Life resumed in a new geographic location, yet for many the game continued.

The air was warm. The sun always shown on a new geographical location. Life was different. Most of all, the music that played everywhere had a flair of enthusiasm. Gilda still remembered the first day she'd descended the steps of the aircraft from Sofia. Hunger overtook her as she made her way through the streets of Mexico City. Trying new foods flared her taste buds with intricate spices that made her eyes water. The young woman received much attention from the opposite sex, mostly because she was alone, which was odd to see. Many questions were asked pertaining to her husband, which were always the same; with the negative response that there was no man to speak of, propositions were posed to her. Always going on her way, she turned them down. In the marketplace, shopping was fresh to her: not just the array of beautiful fruit, but the different clothing that enhanced her figure.

Another beautiful day was on its way. The warm breeze ruffled Gilda's dress as she promenaded along the narrow street approaching a sidewalk café. A voice rang out with a deep, horsy Southern accent. "Hey, lady, do you want to have a drink with me and my partner in crime?"

Her head popped up as she focused her eyes in the bright sunshine. Taken aback for a moment at how the brute of a man enunciated himself, she stood for a moment. His sidekick whistled, full of sexual innuendo. "Come on, sexy."

The first person wailed out, "We got ourselves a bottle of tequila, and that bad hombre over there is going to bring you a glass. There is already a seat waiting for you under this here umbrella—unless you prefer my lap. That would be really nice. You would love it! We even got some tasty food coming. Gilda, it's your favorite dish: spicy rice and beans."

Her thoughts readjusted. "They know my name."

She walked over and sat down. The bad hombre brought her a glass, and then the food arrived. The main question was how they knew her name. She contemplated, "Is this some throwback to Eastern Europe, or is it a sign?"

The two men sat there half-trashed, grinning and chucking. They were middle-aged and had bloated bellies, and they were sweating in the heat of the day. Confident in themselves, there was a projection of their manliness and what they were entitled to. Both were chomping on cigars. Their shirts were unbuttoned, and their hats were on cockeyed. Supposedly, they were some underground characters from another era. Were they only retiring, or were they starting up at a new game?

"Look, gal. I'm Harry, and this is my partner, Lucky. We saw your little song-and-dance routine at the cabaret last night. I do say that you have the most gorgeous legs and the most perfect ass. Oh my, did I ever get a woody! You got some talent, little lady."

Throwing back the shot of tequila, she grabbed the bottle and took a swig. Then, having had enough of the offensive company, she got up to leave.

Harry, without a moment's hesitation, said, "You seem like a real fun gal. Come party with us. We will pay you for your time, little *loca*. We know lots of locals who would love to play with that ass of yours. You could make some really good pesos, honey. Sweet pea, you might find yourself in some interesting company, as long as you put out."

Lucky added to the derogatory comments. "I would love it if you wrapped those legs around my waist. Ha..ha..ha." Lucky laughed so hard that he farted at the same time, followed by a belly burp. Even a playing card—the ace of hearts—fell out of the ribbon on his hat.

A look of repugnance swept over her countenance. Her skin was crawling, as if she had the worst insects all over her. Walking away was what she did. Gilda was getting used to derogatory comments from men. She really did not find any to be respectful. This was an ongoing comedy. There were the same lines over and over again, as if these guys all read from the same script. Worst of all, some would become possessive, as if she were their property.

More time had passed since Gilda spent those many nights working in clubs as an entertainer. Her past life was almost all but forgotten. There were parties and debonair dates. There were even at times flowers. Yet, every day she thought about James in some way and wondered if she was just a convenience who fit into his needs and actions. Then time passed until she met Stephon. He was to become her worst nightmare. Being well acquainted with the underworld, he was buddies with Harry and Lucky.

"That guy," Stephon was an international playboy floating about the world, especially South and Central America. At heart, he was a mama's boy who was in love of course with his mother. Thus, he was incapable of having any respect for anyone, else especially a woman, unless the female was his own mother. If he had to help someone, the person would only be a man. Stephon's moto was that women were to have *nothing—ever*. His arrogance was to the utmost extreme. Women were put on earth solely for a man's pleasure—especially his—and females should be grateful for his manliness! According to his mother, he was the most wonderful and sweetest man ever. The reality was that he was a raging asshole. He was also a drunkard and a drug addict. Stephon was inebriated around the clock, and because he roamed around Central and South America, he got himself some really good drugs. The weed was plentiful, and the coke was fine. The strangeness of this scenario was that he could function in day-to-day life just grand, except for his spats of derogatory comments that he had no control over. There were times when he was nice and cordial. He had social graces, because he was part of the diplomatic community, as was his father. That was just part of the family business. Yet, he always landed a lot of good espionage assignments. The reality was that, even though he was a proficient spy, Stephon was a closeted homosexual who took out his frustrations and jealousy on any unsuspecting females he encountered—mostly because women had a better chance of getting laid with attractive men than he did. The main point was that Stephon especially loved James and most of all was infatuated with the man. He considered himself at the same stature as James, but he was far from having that level of charisma.

Stephon had been friends with James long before he made the acquaintance of Gilda. The two went back years. They were the best of friends. Many of times were spent in discussion over cocktails. At intervals, they enjoyed partaking in nudist get-togethers. Stephon was truly in love with James. The absurd behavior did not stop there. James had been friends with Stephon's family for years, and he even bedded down with Stephon's mother. His father did not seem to mind and was even congratulatory toward James. They were all from affluent families, and etiquette of that nature was all fine. They were people who were above normal senses of conduct; all was fair game, especially with spies, who could sleep with whoever they wanted to.

All in all, Stephon admired James, and he toasted many cocktails in his remembrance. Most of all, he admired how a roomful of people would part ways as

James walked through. His gestures and expression were remarkable. Through osmosis, Stephon believe that because he knew James, he was as great as James. This was not the case. Stephon was a pitiful expression of manhood compared to his superior counterpart. With the notion that Stephon knew James, Stephon had the audacity to imagine that he had the same stature and moxie as James. This was based solely on Stephon's familiarity with a man of such demigod proportions.

James was an exceptional man. He would learn anything new quickly, and he mastered foreign languages with ease. He was a very loving man, but he never stayed to continue any relationships. He did fall in love, but his womanizing was never his fault that he broke hearts. He never hurt anyone; that was all in the woman's delusions. Was it not? Then he always pulled away and went on his merry way. He was nothing but a rolling stone with all the grandiosity that involved; that was his privilege in life. The strange part was that he could fix any situation. His success was such that he was comparable to fictional spy characters with superhuman abilities. As the man he was, James had the pick of any woman on the face of the planet. Some people escape the word "no." This next point was he still a man. At times he would hurt, but not for long. Love was always a brutal emotion that brought down the strongest, who otherwise were left unaffected.

James's counterpart and love interest, Gilda, was a beacon of admiration for people around her and men who wanted to make love to her. Stephon knew that James loved her. This drew him even closer to her, because Stephon wanted control over the ambience. More or less, running the show and using people was Stephon's forte. Stephon's lies were wrapped in insults. He consciously thought he was a nice guy. If he was accused

otherwise, he just thought the accusing person was crazy.

Stephon was Gilda's only connection to the world

and her handler, even though that was never the reality.

No matter his objections to her intelligence, she would

have been lost and without any human direction. When

the rolling stone stopped, the spy was still left with

nothing but the blankness of his existence. A lonely mind

for someone in the espionage community was something

else. Secrets with no donors ravished the clandestine

person's being, because there was no outlet to calm the

mind down. A soothing escape was to be welcomed. The

reality was that the worker was alone, very alone. There

was no one beside the spy, so the spy was left to abject

solitude. Secrets had to be kept at all cost. A weak mind

would go through the meat grinder, but still, one had to

keep their fucking mouth shut. Putting all glamour aside,

the role of an operative really sucked. Many people

became substance abusers, including Stephon.

Chapter 6

The day came in Tijuana, Mexico. It was mid-June, and the air was dry and roasting. This was where Stephon was to make his first acquaintance with Gilda that she was aware of. In actuality, he had been familiar with her for some time by studying her from afar. As any man thought, she had the most beautiful legs and ass ever. This raised the girl to celebrity status throughout South and Central America. Even American businessmen who traveled down south raved of her disposition. Rumor had it, she was the most sensually alluring woman ever. That was how she made her money—by getting guys to fall in love with her. She never had to sleep with anyone unless she wanted to. The manipulative person merely played with her emotions, and in turn she made a tremendous amount of cash, besides gifts and a car. Heading south for the winters was one of the best ideas ever. Besides the warmth of the tropics, it became a lucrative endeavor, even though there was a war going on. She had the freedom to move about.

Gilda left for a drive up the coast in a white Chevrolet Deluxe with a custom paint job. She pushed down the throttle, and the car cruised at eighty miles an hour. She had to pay attention to the crumbling road, yet she was an excellent driver. She tuned the radio for some music before it was out of range, and she mostly heard clicking and scratching over the static that seemed to comprise a pattern.

There was more in the world at war. The mechanisms in men's minds were nothing but mental endeavors to contemplate success with all inherence to duty. In 1942, there were those who held office in the Pentagon for the war department within the Military

Intelligence Service. People were soon to acquire a greater role in Army Intelligence G-2 and, later, the ringleaders of independent contracting intelligence organizations. Many complex reports were recompiled that were based on articles about cryptophone. Cryptophone is the art of sending secret messages over radio broadcast programs.[1] One of these national programs was featured in a military magazine in July 1940. Journal articles were held back from the public for security reasons. What started out as an experiment became the basis for relaying coded messages over the airwaves. The study was also directed toward foreign cryptophone usage. The proposal was given that secret intelligence was to become larger, with fewer limitations

---

[1] "Please Return to Lt. Col. J. V. Grombach Room 2E 740 Pentagon Building," rg. 263, records of the Central Intelligence Agency, p. 12, ARC ID 4509733. "SOP (Field) to Soviet Artillery in the Offensive," the Grombach Organization ("the Pond"), subject and country files 1920–1963. National Archives, College Park, MD.

and faster communications. The Military Intelligence Service worked with the major networks (ABC, NBC, and CBS) to easily pass inconspicuous messages to field agents via phraseology. These messages were transmitted without the knowledge of network personnel. Only a small handful of those involved had any perception.

When a fifth column was formed, this element became the group that undermined another body of people in a targeted county. The perpetrator who formed the offence conducted mental sabotage, because that proceeded any physical attack. The ways in which a fifth column worked were organized and controlled by the national defense programs of the predator country. They targeted the enemy. Some countries were undermined by having fifth columns within their boundaries.

There was inserted a jargon coded message to see if any of the thousand listeners were listening. Authorities noted that a shortwave radio station in Europe transmitted

a signal that was received up to six thousand miles away;

the station emanated a signal prior to its evening

broadcasts that resembled static. In all actuality, it was a

coded message in international Morse code that was sped

up to hide its significance. All cryptograms can be

broken, yet Nazi Germany had a more integrated radio

broadcasting system due to the fact that it was a

totalitarian state that held control of all the stations.

Cryptographic messages were also hidden in music

scores, where the receiver not only had to understand the

cryptogram but also to have a thorough knowledge of

music. At the time, the possibility of monitoring all radio

broadcasts was impossible.

This was all just a very intricate endeavor.

Besides having the right broadcasting equipment,

receivers and decoders were necessary. Code books or

code dictionaries were imperative, yet the memorization by agents in the field was vital to keep the sneakiness. All countries used ciphers, which are a mix of letters, numbers, and symbols that are mixed into a prearranged pattern to be deciphered using a frequency table.

American military concerns were the spread of communism, fascism, and Nazis to both North and South America by the usage of radio propaganda. Hitler was known to have said that the Nazis could create a new Germany in South America. Even in the early 1940s, authorities were alarmed at the members of the American Communist Party gaining positions of power and influence. The Germans certainly used crytophony within their espionage efforts throughout the Americas, allowing them to raise a fifth column.

Gilda did not seem to care about the static on the radio, but she knew it meant something sneaky. She was enjoying the ride and brushed off the fact that she was not trained at reading codes. This was not because she was stupid. She knew that it was not her job to rack her brain that day. The sun was shining, and the wind swept through her long brown mane. She had her sunglasses on and a teal scarf wrapped around her neck that blew in the wind and matched her fashionable dress. The voyage would be a new venture. Before approaching the border of Mexico near Tijuana, she stopped for gas and grabbed a Coke. While drinking the beverage, she noticed how dusty the car had already gotten. The shiny paint had a dull reflection. Come what may, the route by the coast was beautiful, and it could not have been a better day. They knew she was coming.

With an adventurous spirit, Gilda pulled into Tijuana. This was one of many stops dictated through her instructions. She was going to meet someone at Club

Nocturno. When she arrived, she walked through the dusty swinging doors. The poorly lit room reeked of smoke and stale beer. A little sunlight from the entrance cascaded over the wooden shutters. Her eyes had not adjusted yet as she made her way over to a table and ordered a tequila sunrise. At first, she could barely make out the figure on stage, yet there was a strange smell in the air besides the regular bar stench. As she stared, a person was dancing erotically with a rather large boa constrictor wrapped around her. The snake was snuggled around the performer's body. The serpent moved ever so strangely. This was almost hypnotic. The strangest sight was when the snake curled its tail between her legs.

Gilda drank her drink immediately. Feeling stunned that this was where she was supposed to be, she realized that was where she got herself. Her mind was screaming, "How could this be my life?" Alcohol was to become a good companion in her lonely empty life. She ordered another tequila sunrise. In the meantime, the performer made her way through the audience to Gilda. The snake beamed its head up and looked at her at eye level. That was creepy. Her mouth dropped. The Devil was present.

The performer was Maria Garcia, and she asked Gilda in a thick accent, "Do you know Benjamin Franklin?" Gilda almost did not hear her because she was entranced with that snake staring at her with its head bopping up and down, and so close to her face. Gilda thought, rather perplexed, "How could a naked woman with a snake wrapped around her ask me something of such a clandestine nature? What kind of shit is this?"

She responded, "Yes," to the stupid Ben Franklin question.

Maria said, "I have something for you to pass on when you reach your next destination. Come to my dressing room before you leave." And off trotted the snake lady.

After some time passed before Gilda worked up the courage to go back to the snake lady's dressing room. She noticed the door was left slightly open and went in. Fortunately, the snake was in its cage. She was asked to close the door. The two spoke in low voices. Besides the snake lady being utilized in espionage, she had psychic abilities. Breaking out a pack of tarot cards, she told Gilda things of her past and about the sadness of her future. Then, Maria pulled out the package. It was everything that anyone needed to know about who's who in Mexico, including resident foreigners. There were photos and names of people to look out for, most of whom were men. Those were the people who espionage was made for in South America.

Then Stephon showed up in the most grandiose fashion, knocking on the door of the snake lady's dressing room. He seemed to have a thing for short women in general—even better if she came with snakes. On his face was a look of arrogance and a snotty smirk. Gilda obviously fell for the farce. The joke was on her.

Gilda heard a cold, calculating, callous heckle. It was the most insulting laugh anyone could endure. The ridicule was that of an all-knowing person who was far beyond arrogance. The face Stephon made was composed of a sneer that curled his countenance, and his head bobbed from side to side. He said, "Well, well, well. Hello there, Gilda. I see you've met my little friend." Then he laughed some more.

Gilda felt reproached and discredited as she sat in the snake lady's dressing room. She almost wanted to cry, but after all this time she had become more and more desensitized. There were virtually no more feelings left in her to hurt. Except, she felt abject vexation. On the other hand, she could laugh at times, but she was doing no laughing at this point. Her emotions were fading. Too much had happened. She was never considered a human being in the first place—only what she could do for men. If she was a little bit bigger, she would have punched Stephon in the nose. The insults burned her watching his disrespectful expression and listening to the repugnant tone in his voice. What hackled her the most was that he was in control and calling the shots!

Gilda said, "You bastard!"

Stephon, still full of himself and grinning, said, "Come, now, let's go have a drinkie-poo. We have many aspects of your service to discuss."

Gilda asked, "Like what?"

Stephon said, "I am sure you can gather the notion."

The two walked out toward the bar. It was still midafternoon, and the temperature was hot. Light streamed in over the wooden shutters. They pulled themselves up to the bar for some afternoon cocktails. He sat there and smiled at Gilda for a time with that longing gleam in his eye.

Stephon said, "You have done a really excellent job as a sleeper over this past year or so. You need to get busy at working for us harder. All the contacts you made have been phenomenal; you could not have done any better. I'm going to tell you what you're going to be doing under my direction. To start with, more training is at hand in Miami. You did well with my contact person in Mexico City to get this far. That was skillful of you to charm that unsuspecting man out of his car for your transportation, and you did not even have to sleep with him. In addition, he handed over his cash. How persuasive was that? If things were that easy for me, all I would have to do was to bat my eyelashes and smile. People know you, and so many good contacts, even American businessmen, remark on your attributes. Miami is the next place for you, but you have to get there yourself."

Gilda stared at him; his audacity meant that she never had a choice in the matter. Then he informed her that she was to be staying overnight in Tijuana.

She straight out yelled, "I am not sleeping with you, ever!"

Stephon seemed disappointed and finished his drink. Then the doors opened, and in poured Harry and Lucky, grinning from ear to ear. Gilda rolled her eyes in disgust.

Lucky said, "There's that sweet little thing. You're going to be working here and putting on a little show? You'll be a breath of fresh air and the star of Tijuana."

No response came from Gilda. By the time she'd finished her drink, Maria Garcia had come out from her dressing room without her snake, which she called Sam the Boa. Maria headed straight over to Harry and Lucky, jumped up and down with excitement, and gave them both hugs. Maria apparently knew the boys well.

Maria said, "Let's have a party."

So, they did, and Stephon joined them. Gilda collected herself and headed out the door to get a room at a bed and breakfast.

After she'd settled in for the night and had pulled the sheets back, she believed something was not right. She could see little bugs crawling around everywhere. With disgust, she went back downstairs to yell at the innkeeper. When she did, he just looked at her and laughed and refused to give her money back. Storming out, she slammed the door and went back to the club to see Stephon. Strangely enough, they were all still there. Maria got Sam out of his cage. She always had such an emotional attachment to her snake. Sam was perfectly happy to be wrapped around Maria when she was drinking with guys.

Stephon popped his head up and said, "I thought you were turning in for the night because you were too good to be with us."

Gilda said, "The room was infested with bedbugs."

Stephon said, "Oh. Too bad for you. You can bunk with me tonight. My room is clean, and the inn is owned by of friend of mine. We can snuggle."

Gilda was not thrilled, but she nodded her head in approval. Since she was in the cantina, she might as well have another drink. The anticipation was that she would just drift off into a peaceful oblivion. If only she could be in an unconscious state, unaware of what was transpiring.

So, the evening wore on with numerous rounds of drinks. Once the night got late, Stephon and Gilda walked to the inn, with Stephon talking the entire time, mostly about his grandiosity. The "great I am" was his favorite subject. Upon arrival, Gilda crashed out for the night, but Stephon did not seem to sleep. He had some form of insomnia.

Morning came early. When she was getting ready to head out, Stephon said goodbye by calling her his most beautiful friend. He seemed to have some sort of infatuation with her. He walked her to his car and watched her drive off. In a few months, he would rendezvous with her in Montevideo.

Chapter 7

How could that girl possibly get accepted into Army G-2 intelligence school? Somehow, she got drafted. The connection was through observations of her reputation of how fine she was. Stephon was the motivating factor of Gilda's espionage work. He was to profit from the endeavors immensely on a monetary level. As her handler, he benefited both in recognition and control. She made nothing, other than her work in nightclubs. The guy took ownership, possession, and the ultimate mind warp. Gilda was watched over constantly. Before the proposition, her interview began when she did not even know what was transpiring. Before, in Romania, she had already worked as a spy. She never got paid, but she was of the utmost interest.

Florida was a new game, and maybe a new life. She could have pampered herself while drinking Coca-Cola in some fresh surroundings. Gilda was to attend the Army Intelligence School. How she came about this was of the strangest sort. She was not a novice or an unskilled worker of such endeavors. The net just caught her up, and she was pulled through the abysses of meaningless advancement for which team would have the superior outcome.

During this time, she felt abject loneliness. This was an emptiness that was always present. Gilda moved as if she were on some awkward tide. She had no other choice but to go in the movement that presented to her this fate. There was a sadness that resided because she never knew a normal life. In all actuality, many people do not know that luxury. There are some who have the life of a spy as if it is ingrained in them, and as if they were born for that life of espionage. They accept being used.

So, heavy was the weight when she accepted Stephon's proposal. A normal life was out of the question. Somehow, she was brought forward to the understanding that in South and Central America, Nazis were easily ambushed by women. Men were more relaxed and susceptible to female persuasion. There was easy bragging of endeavors. Yet, other than the war in Europe, life was easy and gay. The Germans who resided there were less likely to care about participating in clandestine affairs. They had a newfound sense of life besides the German bullshit of Hitler. Not all Germans adored Hitler. Those who had the money to emigrate did so, either to the Americas or especially to Bern, Switzerland, where they had their own community and diplomats, along with other representatives. Many went to the tropics. Life was good in South and Central America. Their homes were like palaces, and their lives beyond comfortable. There were no frigid climate changes, as was the case in Germany. Whatever transpired in the world, the Nazi Germans who left were but a far reminder of the past. Their newfound reality was not but a welcomed sanctuary free of all German rhetoric. The Nazis of the Americas enjoyed their new lives. And everything they left behind was a dismal reality that had no relevance for the past. They were out of the snake pit. Remarkably, some false loyalty did matter, and did it count. Whatever was relayed to Nazi Germany was of a more mundane disposition. Yet, the threat was still there. Many opted for financial gain, with precious resources that could be mined to turn a profit. There was still an element of danger after an afternoon nap in the heat of the day.

The decision came that Gilda was to get more training. She would leave soon for Florida, where she would   in a compound for a month, although she had to get there by her own means, which is why she picked up the car in Mexico City from an admiring fan. The man would have had a fat pocketbook and a full tank of gas in his car because Stephon was too selfish to give Gilda any of her own money.

Chapter 8

American strategists utilized their resources by brainstorming and thinking out of the norm; this was triggered by the attack on Pearl Harbor. Plans of action were made in place. Weaknesses were evaluated, and the Americans proposed an intricate worldwide network to protect the interests of the United States. First and foremost, the Special Intelligence Branch was structured under the backing of the Chief of Staff's office on May 16, 1942. Setting up a spy network took time, which was conducive to ingenuity with considerable devising. Once again, time was the factor. The mobilization of inexperienced staff members and systems came about with considerable training of staff or otherwise intense work. The main purpose was to get people in the right locations to be the most useful. The Military Intelligence

Division, especially in Latin America, was wide open with options to get workers in the field. The notion had showed that a few months into the war there was a need for more reconnaissance activity. The idea was to guard the Panama Canal area. The emphasis was that there had been no centralized intelligence prior to 1947. Pertinent information gathering by the army, navy, and FBI was all done by separate components that did not necessarily interact nor share insight among the various governmental groups.

"The times are precarious," Colonel Harrison thought to himself over his morning cup of coffee at his desk in the compound of the Army Intelligence School. As he was finishing his coffee, he tapped his pencil on his desk. He was thinking. Mulling over in his mind how to improve on training instruction. He wanted his people to be successful, since their lives depended on it.

The office window was open. A car pulled up, and a person got out and slammed the door. Colonel Vance approached the compound with a stack of folders clenched in one arm and his briefcase in the other. Vance had just come back for the Pentagon in DC.

Harrison greeted him with a hello and said, "Did you survive the maze of the Pentagon's corridors? Navigation in those quarters is quite tough."

Vance came in and plopped the folders down on the table. He said, "I managed. We got some good ones this time. There is a whole smorgasbord of the most offbeat personalities. There are even a few career criminals. They have the temperament for clandestine work and lived abroad in Latin America for some prolonged stints. We got to try whatever works. People with an underground nature in the past have been more successful."

Harrison added, "Many South American countries were already affected by Nazism, and they leaned toward the Germans."

Vance said, "Yeah, I know. So, I did some revision on the training program. We should be up to snuff with the approach the British use. The recruits will learn the actual operations of covert work. We can produce some of the best spies. That's why we are going to expand the training to six weeks."

Harrison said, "Let me see those files." He walked over to the table and started sorting through them. They were synopses of all the recruits and attached photos. "Oh, we got two women this time. That's going to be a pain in the backside."

Vance added, "They are both very different. One gal is middle-aged, and the other one is a nightclub entertainer. We can make our assumptions."

Harrison held up Gilda's photo for a few moments. He was fond of young, charismatic women.

Vance interjected, "She has this most incredible ass. Here's a picture."

"Oh, really. Wow! Look at that!"

"Yeah. It's to die for."

"Is she a prostitute?"

"No, Gilda is just proficient at manipulating men with no exchange of sex. They give her whatever she wants. She was even involved with James Benson for a bit."

"James Benson? Really?"

Vance nodded his head and smiled. He was actually really hot for her. The guy was unable to get her off his mind. "We will give her an assignment nowhere near him." He laughed and added, "We will place the right agents in the right location, like playing a game of chess. There are going to be no love scenarios during this war."

Then the two officers had a good prolonged chuckle.

Vance announced, "Just to let you know, I found out who is going to be running the show in South and Central America from now on. It's Colonel Walter Jones. He's coming to Miami in a few days."

"You don't say. Did you know that his father was a diplomat? There had to have been some real spying going on in that family. It's not uncommon that when parents work in the clandestine field, their offspring follow suit."

Vance said, "That guy can throw a mean left hook, you know. I saw that when he was working in the military police in the Panama Canal Zone."

"That's because he was an Olympic boxer back in the day."

A FEW DAYS PASSED. Colonel Walter Jones show up at the Army Intelligence School. He was tired from the drive down from DC. Disgruntled, he greeted the other officers and asked to be shown to his room, where he showered and changed before dinner. There was much dialogue during the meal. He said, "This organization is to counterbalance the OSS, because the guy running it, General Sid, is incompetent. I tell you!" Walter had issues with anyone else who was running a spy network besides the FBI. He had a good working relationship with those boys. "You can't believe the asinine things General Sid does. I have no idea how he survives being such an idiot." Walter was simply a harsh critic when he felt there was a threat to him from the enemy. "We need another name for this organization. There are even guys who know how to make money work; they have international banking expertise. That comprises a whole financial section of the Special Intelligence Branch. Shady transactions can be detected by our boys, or the movement of crucial material. We can spot them out, and the FBI can round them up in South and Central America. Even the postal and cable service will be monitored. Is that not grand?"

Vance nodded his head. He'd heard this spiel a few times, especially the mantra about General Sid.

Walter continued, "Everything is in our grasp. The Germans are projecting their military strategy, primarily toward Russia. The Japanese fleet took a hard hit with their carriers in the battle of Midway, which reduced the possibility that they will use Kamikaze plans to attack the Panama Canal. The Allied offensive in

Africa is deterring the Axis forces from jumping across the Atlantic to attack Panama."

Harrison attentively listened and asked, "Operations more tailored to the changing climate of the war, especially in our division."

Walter interjected, "There is such an influx of refugees who are involved in espionage. So, it's important that information be gathered on them. There are just so many damned thieves everywhere! Everywhere you look, there they are! And the propaganda the Nazis turn out is abundant. Those bastards!"

In 1942, there was not a sense of interagency cooperation. They were not always able to get information through other agencies; adaptions were made in reference to gaining insight.

Harrison commented, "Why can't we all just get along?"

Walter grunted without answering. Then he added, "We have some good agents coming out. We can determine the risk that they will face based on their training. I believe that so much more information could be extracted by the usage of secret sources than that which are overt. Guys, this one is in the bag. We got it even though we had no groundwork prior to this war."

Vance said, "We have the right methods of selecting agents. They are observed and judged, even before the initial approach."

Harrison said, "Yeah, they will be able to move about certain social circles. Their covers will be exactly what the agents intend to project. A certain temperament of person will be recruited for a designated type of cover. They will learn how to relay their work through the embassy to get to the military attaché for the vehicle to relay to the States."

Vance continued, "We used some sneaky detective work to get connected with people who have ties to Latin American contacts and have had extensive experience there."

Walter asked, "Which was?'

Vance replied, "Anyone traveling South of the border was observed."

Harrison said, "That is about the gist of our work. Most people are willing to serve their country, including foreigners who want to take refuge with us."

Walter said, "I see."

Harrison said, "The problem is that some people talk and blow their cover. They just cannot keep a secret. Then we have to relocate them to work in a different country or pull them from the field altogether if the really made a fucking ass out of themselves."

Vance added, "It is so much work for us to resituate an agent. If only they'd stick with their training. They lose focus, or they have some sort of superiority complex where they feel they have to brag. God damn those bastards!"

Walter said, "Well, on a lighter note, we always have the fairer sex. Even though this profession is mostly men, we are getting quite a few female candidates. They can do the job pretty well at half the pay. They seem to understand the Espionage Act and are able to swear to an oath of secrecy. I think our girls will do just fine. Besides, they smell delightful. Those OSS people, or Sid with his brainstorming, even have their girls parachuting behind enemy lines to work. Imagine that woman power working over those Nazis. Their girls are quite successful. We can do just as well or even better. And no one will ever know that women were the muscle of this machine."

Harrison said, "Let's call it a night. We have a group arriving on Sunday."

At the beginning of the unpleasant journey, the recruits were made to sign an oath not to disclose their association with the Military Intelligence Division. Some of the difficulties were that the person was not able to confide in anyone with the necessity of keeping secret and being isolated. In addition, the agent had to memorize his directive given by the coverage officer, who has the instruction on a single copy, which was later stored at the Secret Intelligence Branch headquarters. Interestingly enough, in some undisclosed location, these records must still be intact of all the agents' missions, which set the precedent for all intelligence agencies. The agent was basically a lone player in the foreign country he was working in. If he had issues with officials, no agency would help, and the Military Intelligence Division would deny any and all connection with its agent. He was to maintain his cover, no matter what. Does this actually sound like a glamorous job? Why would someone put themselves in this position?

THE ARRIVAL CAME SOON ENOUGH. The guys were well kept and clean cut. They rolled in early on Sunday afternoon. Then Harry and Lucky showed up much later in the day. They were met by the instructional commander in the front of the compound. Lucky threw down his bag at the feet of the instructor and gave a big, "How do you do?"

Harry laughed with a superior attitude, offending the commander, Smith. Smith yelled, "Pick up your bags and get inside, now!"

Harry and Lucky were still smirking like bad children.

When the time was reaching nightfall, Gilda drove up in her car. She was feeling thirsty, and she wished she had stopped for a Coca-Cola when she had the chance. Sitting for a minute before she got out of her car she collected her thoughts, brushed her hair, and put on some fire-red lipstick. This was added with a dash of perfume. The door of the compound opened, and officer Jones came to her car with the warmest greetings. He asked, "Can I help you with your bags?"

Graciously she accepted his offer to help. He escorted her into the compound. Jones added, "Dinner will be served soon. There are several recruits already waiting in the courtyard. No one here goes by their real name. Do you remember that from the memo we sent you?"

Gilda replied, "No. Stephon would not let me have the paper. He said he was going to keep the document in a safe place."

Jones said, "You don't say. Stephon was always such a callous person to deal with. I always hated having to work with him. Just think of a name you want to use when you talk to the others. There are some people you might already be acquainted with."

There was a group of about twenty, in addition to Harry and Lucky. Gilda saw them and just about cringed. The rest of the guys looked her up and down.

Frank said, "Look at the legs on her that form a perfect ass. I would like to spoon her."

Scott replied, "She does not have much of a chest."

Frank interjected, "That does not matter. Her ass is unbelievable!"

Joyce overheard the conversation and did not like what Frank and Scott were saying. Her face formed a scowl of disgust. She thought derogatory comments in her head. Most of all, she was offended that Gilda would show up wearing such a short skirt. The cloth was so thin that the garment was almost translucent. Joyce's brain was screaming, "She is doing nothing but flaunting her body. I am even going to have to share a room with her for the next month!"

They went into the dining hall. Gilda stayed clear of Harry and Lucky. That night she ate her meal by herself. Not feeling any connection with anyone, she preferred to keep quiet. The evening passed.

Chapter 8

Miami Beach, Florida, on any given day had the breeze from the ocean. There was a spell where the air was stale and murky, which made sleeping a sticky endeavor. Before the sun came up, the temperature had already risen. There was even an abundance of insects not much different than in the tropics. Snores from the adjoining rooms reverberated throughout the building. Those were sounds that most women cannot stand; this leads to sleep deprivation from the nightly echoes of stuffed-up nostrils. There were not many women in the compound that month for training. Only two of the fairer gender occupied a room by sharing space for nighttime slumber. The rest of the house was filled with a bunch of guys with all levels of education and expertise. Somehow the smorgasbord cohabited for a whole isolated month. The chances of getting off the grounds was slim unless chaperoned on one of the Sunday afternoons. This was in all probability not going to happen. So, hopes became disappointment, shadowed by the seriousness of that level of commitment. It was important that they absorb all the curriculum and not prance around South Florida.

On one of the mornings at the Army Intelligence School compound, the gong went off at 4:00 a.m. The syllabus read that the gong was supposed to go off at exactly 7:00 a.m. The sound penetrated the building and made the snoring off-key with a slowing of the snorts. No affect was rendered, so it rang again and again, stirring the cadets to pull themselves out of restful sleep and turn on the lights. So, the day began early, even for the guys with military training, who would also miss the additional rest. Gilda thought to herself, "You got to be kidding me." Then she got dressed in her workout clothing and pulled her hair back into a bun on top of her head, which made her look ever so goofy. They proceeded to start the day. There was still quite a bit of material to cover, hence the early-morning rise. Physical fitness was always at the beginning of the structured day. This entailed a three-mile run.

This was a crash course in which they had to absorb material in a limited amount of time. The entire day was rigidly structured with a range of important topics. Of course, there was time for meals in the syllabus also. There was even time scheduled in the evenings for studying. Some of the classes were about the Nazi underground in Latin America, and the Nazi modus operandi, or the way they do things. The usage of poisons, propaganda, wiretapping, and clandestine radio were quite interesting. Because of the threat, the Japanese lecture filled a two-hour block of time. Map reading and sketching were also on the docket. Information about various countries in South and Central America was used to explain the difference in culture and why many people leaned toward favoring the Nazis. A view of the effects and advancement of communism was exposed early on.

There was just a little sexism going on. There were just two females. Not more in the prior class composed of women. In all actuality, much of the staff of G-2 and the OSS was composed of ladies. They just did not get as much credit nor recognition as their male counterparts. Even one guy labeled Gilda as the thinking man's bimbo.

Joyce and Gilda were teamed up during the segment for hand-to-hand combat, which was insufficient training for taking on a big guy. Being an older woman in her forties, Joyce did not easily accept Gilda. There were the glares and eye-rolling that had to be contended with.

Besides, the younger of the two got more attention from the guys; she piqued their interest, and they were left with the feeling of being hot. She created some stress in the compound because she was a distraction and the sexiest thing around. She lost count of the evenings when she got propositioned by a study partner who, in a short amount of time, got very handsy. Joyce really got sick of Gilda with her sex appeal, so she was met with scowls and a disapproving disposition. Gilda was left with no choice but to go about her charming way.

Training was successful, and the new spies assumed their positions south of the border.

The instructors did a rather efficient job with training Army Intelligence School AIS agents, because only a small handful were detected. Gilda was not one of them. No one suspected her. Eighty-four agents were sent out up until October 1943. Six agents were exposed by other US government agencies. Only one was identified by the Nazis. To the best of their knowledge, the Latin American population did not expect any of the AIS agents, or if they did, no alarm was raised. There were more agents in the field who did not go through AIS training.

Gilda's cover was that of an entertainer who danced and sang for men in nightclubs. Why not use this to her advantage, when she had her youth on her side? In all respects, Gilda was envious of Joyce, whose cover was that of buyer for various department stores.

Joyce was already a buyer for a department and specialty story. She had already frequented Mexico and Brazil. Prior to her AIS training, she was well established with various contacts who were friends and business associates. With the onset of the war, she went into the Women's Army Auxiliary Corps but was released because she was above the age cutoff. Her cover was that of a buyer looking for unique merchandise for Macy's, Woodward and Lothrop, and B. Altman and Company. She started working for the AIS in 1942 then reported to the military attaché in Brazil on April 2, 1943. Joyce was overridden with moxie when she engaged in questioning a Pan Am representative about the consulate in Columba. Her actions as a spy were too direct, and the FBI, Office of Naval Intelligence, and state department flagged her, although she never exposed her connection with the Military Intelligence Service Thus, she was still deemed a good agent and was transferred to Mexico to continue her assignment, where she did exemplary work.

Joyce was taken so much more seriously and respected as an older woman who had gone through military intelligence. Everyone else was taken so much more seriously, along with Harry and Lucky, who were former rumrunners during the Prohibition years.[2] There were also agents who were well versed in underworld activities where their expertise was also beneficial, yet not without some drawbacks. Harry and his partner in crime Lucky were former rumrunners during Prohibition times. Harry was quite familiar with the coast of Mexico, and Lucky had lived there for twenty years. They moved easily with the subversive circle and were suitable for clandestine work. Harry was even commissioned by the ONI for some time before the AIS was established. He was advised not to reveal any connection the Military Intelligence Division, yet an ONI officer who knew him confronted him in Vera Cruz. With some pressure, he revealed his connection to MIS. This information was spread widely through ONI and MID. Harry was brought back to the States. During his next stint in Mexico, he had some reports that he secured, and he had difficulties bringing them through customs. A notion was made; this was due to his friendship with a customs inspector, although the customs inspector notified military intelligence, and Harry was once again pulled. As a result, both Harry and Lucky were bought to the United States for AIS training. They returned with the cover of being cattle dealers, since they are known to avoid the law. Then the two were sent to California, and because Harry had a record as a former rumrunner, he was picked up by the FBI. When released, he was called back to the AIS and was fired. Harry then spent time in military service in the South Pacific, and not in the intelligence field.

Agents who exposed their cover were retained by AIS in some diminished position. That was the protocol that British intelligence followed: the agent was retained and kept on a secret roster. If it was no fault of their own, they were reassigned to another country to carry on clandestine work, because there was already an investment in developing these people, and they could still be useful by gaining from their experience. In contrast, agents who exposed themselves by their own doing were scrutinized. It was thought that they would continue to speak freely about their operations, when indeed they let others know that they were spies. In keeping with the war effort, they were confined for the duration of the war. These agents took an oath of secrecy to never reveal their connection to MID and were disassociated with any connection to the agency. For the agents, there was an air of seriousness that their deliberate announcement of their espionage activities would be prosecuted under the Espionage Act.

The group was an interesting and diverse bunch. All of them were to be working in South and Central America as well as many other places.

Chapter 9

After training, Gilda went straight to Montevideo,

Uruguay, which was across the Rio de la Plata from

Buenos Aires. Rarely did she get a soft bed to sleep in. At

times, she had to contend with bedbugs, waking up in the

middle of the night and itching profusely. She got a great

tan in the tropics over the top of her bedbug rash. The

best was that the fresh fruit was in abundance, and the

rich sweetness tasted full of life. She could forget she was

in a strategic location and had to work. Little escapes

were always welcomed.

Uruguay was a country rich in oil, minerals, and

bauxite. Arms shipments also went through the port of

Montevideo as well as Buenos Aires, heading in the

direction of North Africa. Germans were already planted

throughout South America who were more than willing to

support the Reich in any way possible. They were also there for backup, just in case everything fell to hell with the Nazi endeavor. In other words, their contact people were already located throughout the underground social network.

Having coverage in Latin America was important for the MID in the early part of 1942. The Germans already controlled much of North Africa west of Egypt. The port of Dakar, Senegal, was a strategic location for German offensives toward Latin America. US intelligence was ill-prepared when entering the war. The original AIS agents were quickly chosen and trained, which posed some drawbacks. The evolution of the AIS observed past practice and improved upon the future training and employment of prepared agents. The priority was that the MID and AIS would get agents in the center of Axis citizens and agents with pressing urgency. They needed to place enough agents to establish a communication net via local citizens as informers. Their ideal agents were people who were already long-term residents of Latin America and had friends there whom they had known for years.

By 1943, there was a sense of success with the network. There were not all that many agents working; they were the sum between the military attaché and AIS-employed agents. The perception at the time was that their people were not as suspected by German intelligence, the Latin Americans, and other US governmental entities. The AIS started out with fewer than one hundred agents to cover from Mexico to the southern tip of Chile. Somehow, six got flagged right away by other US agencies. This was an issue during that time, because the various branches of the military and the FBI had the world carved up in terms of who was in power in which territory and especially in their territory. One poor fellow just reeked for attention to the Germans. Yet in the initial stages of the operation, there was no attention drawn by the Latin Americans, or so they thought, or maybe people chose to look the other way. The military attachés were well established; there were 505 of them in the field at work. Three military attachés were flagged by other agencies (primarily the FBI), which had the most vested interest in Latin America. They owned the place, and that was their domain. Although in Haiti, one military attaché was exposed. The percentages were extremely low on who got caught. There were 1.53 percent suspected by the other agencies that Special Intelligence Branch as aware of, and 0.34 percent suspected by the Nazis and Latin Americans that they were aware of. All Americans in Central and South America could have fallen under suspicion. This could have given the SIB unfounded security. The consideration was that if an agency was aware of a SIB agent, he or she was thought to no longer be of service due to the exposure, because this could have been presented to the Nazis and native Latin Americans. All and all, they saw themselves as a successful bunch in South and Central America.

No matter what was transpiring, Central and South America was still beautiful. The warm sea air drifted into town. At times, the smell of fish being brought onto the docks permeated the air. Montevideo, Argentina saw a frenzy of the influx of people on the streets and elsewhere during Carnival, besides the daily arrival of Europeans. The air was full of anticipation of days of fun-filled partying. Nightclubs and casinos were overwhelmed with the prospect of newfound companionship. The festivities brought more Nazis into the arena, along with everyone else having a gay time.

The festivities were always a delightful experience, especially when there was a war going on. At times such as Carnival, no one could know what was in store. There were so many bizarre instances that took place.

One such unusual person was the warlord arms dealer Herr Tötung, who traveled between Buenos Aires and Montevideo frequently. Originally, he was a baron from Germany who had settled in Argentina and had business dealings and property in Uruguay. Among the festivities, he had business to attend to. He was making money—a lot of money. Tötung was to meet other German confidants whom he'd had prior relations with; they were the vehicle for supplying arms. One manufacturing plant in Argentina was mostly used to serve the Axis in North Africa. Getting rich was all but certain. He enjoyed the underground activities immensely. The warming power was enough to gather control and superiority. Most of all, he enjoyed the lifestyle and the women he attracted even though he was an older man with silver hair. His stunning disposition drew enemies. This type of man was not to be treaded upon. Most of all, he provoked fascination with his deep and seductive voice.

Herr Tötung was not working for free with any disdainful ideology. Nazis paid the most, and he gave them the most assistance—not for love of the Reich, but for the downright grubby cash that would come in endless abundance. Bank accounts were set up in the Americas for the transfer of funds. The war baron was in his glory.

For years, Herr Tötung worked as a mercenary and a soldier of fortune. He partook in many campaigns in Africa. Bloodbaths were always in his wake. For whatever reason, he enjoyed the kill. He found glee in how easy the termination was. Murdering people was as simple as cutting a straw in comparison to a jugular vein. Herr Tötung really loved to dispose of people in all kinds of diverse ways. Slandering individuals was completely accepted if this was for money. Nothing about executions ever bothered him. One of his favorite things to do was to cut off a person's eyelids so the victim would have to suffer for the rest of his life by constantly having to hold a wet rag to their eyes. He would be welcomed into hell on red blood carpets with all the pleasures of the underworld.

Herr Tötung found himself in the companionship of Gilda once again. She was the breath of fresh air. Herr Tötung met with her when he was in the center of Montevideo, checking on a club of his. This was not in the same fashion as sophisticated nightclubs with a casino. The establishment was more subdued. There was a bar with food to be served and of course entertainment.

The German warlord, Herr Tötung, had a fancy for Gilda. For a time, he let his guard down. Gilda ended up being drawn to him. He said, "Maybe I should break out the arm and leg shackles. A certain level of pain could be quite pleasurable." She quickly declined the proposition but enjoyed his company anyway. "I have the highest body count on the continent." There was a provocative fascination with him, and admiration. And the days moved on.

Later in the marketplace on a particular day, James was there. She thought his presence was peculiar because she was just shopping for fruit. Seeing him in a marketplace in Montevideo was so unbecoming. As he touched her on the arm, an electrical current ran through her that penetrated every cell of her body. The smile on his face contrasted with the sadness in his eyes. Then he walked away into the crowd of busy onlookers. Only the melody of a lone man playing Spanish guitar attracted her focus. His fingers moved in a weepy fashion. Then she turned and continued shopping. He just wanted to see her. She stopped for a time in the marketplace and wept like a baby.

James was a man of extraordinary proportion who rarely gave out his heart; love was of a lesser quantity. Yet he did fall in love, as a rolling stone could rest on a plateau for a moment before falling down a blackened chasm or a deep fissure in the earth. When he fell, enchantment consumed him. That was all that he brought in the light of the universe, and his moxie was always in the light. The strange part was that he could right any situations. The magic was through his veins. As the man he was, James commanded through time and all dimensions. Some people escape gravity, logic, and all boundaries. For this next point, he was still a man with emotions and tender thoughts. He was nevertheless hurt at the weakest point, as love was always a brutal emotion that brought down even the strongest, who otherwise predominated. As deeply as he always loved her, his interest reflected depth and despair in his absence. His counterpart engaged in destructive scenarios. People, places, and times prevented love from growing and becoming the divinity it was. Nothing was the sort in a violent world where borders were to be protected, and emotions were irreverent. Love had no place in a world where there were killing centers to liquidate whole families and anyone else who was deemed disposable.

At that point forward, Gilda had no one else but her handler, who was of course in love with her. He was her only connection to the world. Her life was a lie, yet when it came down to it, she had no one else. He was her only outlet from the isolation that surrounded her entirely. The relentless nature was to fabricate all responses pertaining to various scenarios. This was the constant throughout the days. An incorrect response was detrimental. It became second nature to entangle the truth with fiction. Some truth woven among utter fiction was so smooth and effective for various endeavors. Lies coupled with truth were believable.

Somehow the girl looked forward to infinite possibilities. The catalyst of constantly moving gave her hope. All the personal sacrifices that were a well-accepted notion just broke through to the infinite. Nothing was lost in the moment of a life that took place in the millisecond of an existence such as that of a spy. Day-to-day life brought a daily high, with unexpected events; besides, one never knew what was to come next.

When she was kind, there was an air of compassion. By contrast with others' benevolent approach, she was taken aback at their soft behavior, because this was confusing and so usual. Yet, she had a real sharp temper which she had commenced in Sofia. Her costumes were custom-made, and her hair and makeup were always done to perfection. As always, her ass was God's gift to men, whether she liked it or not. So, what happened? She got real sick of the indecent propositions with those grimy hands on her. Derogatory comments were common in the club. Being treated as a stupid whore tormented her mind. Being hammered by insults, especially from the other girls, made her hate life even more. At times, the other entertainers poured slimy water from the kitchen on her street clothing and jacket. Stephon was her only connection to the world, even though that was never reality. No matter his abrasiveness, she would have been lost without any human direction. When the rolling stopped, and a spy was still present, they were left with

nothing but the blankness of their existence. A lonely

mind for a person in the espionage community was

something else. Secrets with no donors ravished the

clandestine person's being, because there was no outlet to

calm the mind. A soothing escape was to be welcomed.

The reality was that the workers were alone, very alone.

There was no one beside them and themselves with abject

solitude. Secrecy had to be kept at all cost. Placing all

glamour aside, the role of an operative really sucked.

Many people became substance abusers.

In every conversation between Stephon and Gilda,

the world revolved around Stephon, because he was the

center of the Earth. He was the only topic, and he only

talked of himself and his prospects. As it goes, one is

supposed to always eat shit unless raised to an upper level

of importance. He would say to Gilda, "You're a real cool little chickee, but you are disposable."

When Gilda was going to visit with the war baron Tötung, Stephon said, "Oh, you are in contact with him. Tell him I would do anything to help him because of who I am." Stephon would never help Gilda; at most, he made her life more difficult. He only helped men. She was nothing, but a glorified sex slave used and meant to be discarded. Never was she to dispute the scenario. That was the way: she never mattered in the beginning or end. The fact of being disposable was clear.

Chapter 10

In the community, personal sacrifice was a well-accepted notion. Looking forward to the act of seeking adventure gave people hope and the prospect of infinite possibilities. Despair and boredom were left to the wayside. There was the excitement and intrigue, besides the fascination of living on the rocky precipice. Life was more worth living when there was an element of danger before plunging off the edge because that was more fun. There was no place for depression when one could lose one's life at any moment. The threat of death gave people the passion and desire to live life to the fullest while on the verge of a nothing. Booze was a common companion.

Callous indifference and atrocities were what the world was comprised of. In the grand scheme of things, her life did not matter, nor did anyone else's. The world was all about liquidating underdogs. Hate was the unforgiving gospel. Killing was acceptable, because there was a selection of human beings who never mattered in the first place. Stealing was a state institution. Stress was in abundance as blank pages were presented. There was only getting by on one's own resources. Never did she have the right to protest or say anything on her behalf, because she was a woman. This was a man's world, for men to do as they pleased. Avoiding conflict, the bystander never saved the day. Most of all, personal feelings did not have a place in a violent world. This was the norm for much of the planet. She thought, "Maybe at the end of my life I will just be thrown in a ditch and left to die."

This was a mistake that she had no control over. Dealing with crude people became second nature. At what point do people make the biggest mistakes in their lives? In turn, never in her life was she treated with respect. She was an unpaid spy because she was working off the books. At times, she forgot she was involved in espionage because she was so submerged and under the radar. Most of the time she just could not remember the role she played. The girl was nothing but that of a toy doll with a string in her back. When it was pulled, the person who pulled it would hear exactly what they wanted to hear. When she did not display her nice little doll expression, there were always profound consequences to pay. In the grand scheme of things, she never mattered. When it came down to it, she had no one. There was no rock to hold on to and a world full of people who only cared about themselves. People were exceedingly shallow. How important was standing out in a crowd? Being the most beautiful never mattered. There was an emptiness and isolation. She felt she could not do that anymore. No one ever wanted her to speak her mind. After all, she was female, and she was getting mean.

This was one of the most glorious mornings. Gilda was awakened by the afternoon sun on her skin after sleeping peacefully. Finally, after some months, the bedbugs had dissipated. During her sleep, Herr Tötung had sent flowers, fruit, and a gift card that read, "Come to my home for an afternoon delight." She became supersonically sensitive and ecstatic. Quickly, she bathed and arranged her hair simply with a modest touch of makeup. Full of anticipation, she could not wait to leave her flat. Walking along the colonial district, she was full of smiles and radiance. Reflecting on how great the afternoon would go, she hurried along the corridors. Close to the inlet, she came close to Herr Tötung's villa. The appearance was warm and inviting. She opened the gate and climbed the steps to the front door. She knocked ever so sweetly, and the door was soon answered by Tötung's man. Gilda was welcomed back with all sweetness. There were fresh figs on the table beside a bowl of nuts. A lot of nuts that need to be cracked.

Then Tötung appeared in the doorway. She came toward him. Shoving her face into the wall, he tied her hands behind her back and pushed her toward the open door, where his boat driver was waiting with a guest: Frans VonBrutal. She approached with dread with every footstep. There was Frans VonBrutal standing next to Herr Tötung. Grabbing her by the arms, they took her out back to Tötung's private dock for a little boat ride. VonBrutal still had his dangerous sex appeal. He was good looking and dashing as usual, but deadly. Very deadly. She was abruptly thrown into the boat, knocking the wind out of her. This left her breathless and gasping for air. They got her and caught on to what she was doing. She had stolen enough documents from Tötung to fill a filing cabinet. They contained names and places and much pertinent information. It was a list of all the Nazi operatives in South America and their activities. These documents were read in a hurry, and she never noticed VonBrutal's name on the register. Then Tötung's driver pulled away from the dock with the jolting of the waves of the shallow inlet.

VonBrutal, opportunist that he was, went to South America. He had no desire to fight on the Eastern Front, so he went south. That for him was an easier campaign. Besides, he could make more money and have more uncomplicated work with pleasure. Life was effortless in South America where he could live as a king—which was what he thought he was in the first place.

As the boat driver pulled away from the North bank of the Rio de la Plata, Gilda gasped for air, which made Tötung smile. She asked, "Do you really have to do this?"

They both chuckled, and even the boat driver seemed to be laughing. Gilda hated being laughed at— that made her blood boil even in the face on intimidate death.

Tötung said, "Maybe you should have thought of this before you had such sticky fingers. No one crosses me, ever. I'm going to add you to my body count."

She was to be shark bait, because she was nothing but a piece of meat for those men. Gilda screamed out, "I do not owe any man anything!" This was a defiant stance she took. The notion was mostly meant for her former Nazi boyfriend, who suddenly came back to life. Somehow at the brink of death, she still knew she was a normal human being. Her life went from entertaining to completely and utterly disturbed. She made every move possible as if doves were to fly out from between her legs.

VonBrutal screamed at her as chum was thrown into the water, "Do you really want to die for this scenario? Woman, what are you thinking to be in cahoots with those Americans?"

She kept silent but continued to make eye contact, knowing that at this point, she was at the complete and utter end. She was doomed. Things in her life always went from one extreme to another.

Sharks were circling through the chum. She was actually going to die on that perfect peaceful afternoon. The sea was calm, and the ocean's current was delightful. A soft breeze rippled through her hair. Yet the sharks' fins had such an ominous presence. What does one do when all hope is gone? Prayers are to no avail. Begging and pleading would be nothing but pathetic and meek.

Self-reliance is all that's left to the person who is capable of using it and has the moxie to do so when there is no backup and Prince Charming has no intention of saving the day for his damsel in distress.

VonBrutal shoved her toward the edge of the boat. She saw the sharks' heads popping in and out of the water. With her arms pulled behind her, she leaned toward the water. VonBrutal said, "Look at how your precious James is going to remember you. Do you think he will actually shed a tear on your behalf? Where is he?"

"I do not know. At this point, no one cares. Please do not kill me. I beg you not to do this," said Gilda.

At that moment, VonBrutal pulled her arms toward him. She was never so scared. She couldn't remember the last time she had peed herself. A warmth came from her upper thighs, more or less between them, and that low point of her peeing herself was when action was taken. With her hands still tied behind her back, the talented young lady once again grabbed hold of dear old VonBrutal's pistol and shot him. So, she thought in her mind which was projected into the astral plane or otherwise other dimension. This time dead, or so she thought. As he hit the deck from behind, she shot enough bullets to kill Tötung. As she cut her ropes with a deck knife, the boat driver asked, "Where would you like to go, my lady?" The girl had a resourceful disposition when necessary. Women have survival instincts as much as men.

That was what Gilda thought in her mind that transpired but did not occur. Both VonBrutal and Tötung had themselves a good chuckle. They projected their thoughts which made clear she was to be obedient with all servitude. VonBrutal Screamed at Gilda, "Do you understand? Now!"

Chapter 11

Underground people are simply a different bread of cat.
Personal sacrifice was a well-accepted notion, but they
had fun in the bending of reality. At most, there was no
time to pay attention to useless emotions. There was
excitement and intrigue, besides the fascination of living
on the edge. Activities that hold an air of danger are often
more fun.

After the war, Gilda never went back to Romania
for whatever reason, but when she drank, she was able to
forget about her life. This was not just because the
Soviets had taken over and inflicted the population with
communism. Life there had its problems even before the
war. Her family put her to work serving drinks and
preparing food, and then they took all the money she

earned, even though she was no longer living in their house.

At the end of the war, Gilda ended up living in the Washington, DC, suburbs. The area was very nice, with well-kept homes that the owners took pride in. The war was over, and many people tried to resume their mundane existences, with dinner at five o'clock right on schedule. One of the most amazing things was that in the DC area, she was treated as someone important. Many times, she could not believe how gracious the people were who treated her with respect. Gilda had a reprieve in life that she embraced full of gratitude.

DC was where she got a job working as a waitress in a quaint diner in her neighborhood. The people who came into the diner were very nice, and they asked how her life was in the most caring fashion. The job was what she needed to pay the rent and the commodities of day-to-day life. This was good because she really did not have much money saved from her work during the war. Surviving was pricey, and she spent the money as she earned it. Most of all, her ticket to the United States had been pricey. Finding a place to stay took the last of her funds.

She never considered marriage, because signing that type of contract was not of any interest to her. She did not want to be exclusively used. The thought of taking care of a man and raising his children was unthinkable to her. That would have been just another form of slavery. There would be giving even when she had nothing left to give. A lifetime of servitude would whittle her down to nothing. Gilda had had enough practice with men. Feeling worn out, she felt that retiring would be fine with her.

Occasionally, she had a date who bought dinner which was good especially when she had a week in which she was broke. There were those occasions when she was expected to flop on her back for a plate of food as if she were a cheap whore. Gilda never felt that she had to deliver the package, nor did she fall for that nonsense. She never owed any man anything even for a plate of food.

Then she met Derrick Washington. That guy was dashing and clever. The man possessed a flair for self-confidence that derived from his own affirmations of the self-made man. He was quite a stunning individual with chiseled features and well-kept blond hair. He even made a point of exercising daily, and his physique was quite nice. Each morning, he did one hundred push-ups. He had the stature of a social mover or a man who could move mountains. Most of all, he said straight out that he was an intelligence officer.

Without any warning, he complained that Gilda had let her ass go, which was supposed to be God's gift to men. He was even kind of angry about Gilda's frumpy ass. Derrick said, "How could you do that?"

She did not even respond to his out-of-line behavior. Her ass still looked fine.

Some time passed after their first meeting. It was a few months. Gilda just had that feeling that something was very wrong, because she was haunted by her past associations from South America. A call was made. Derrick Washington answered. She said, "I think that someone is going to kill me."

"Call the police!"

She knew full well that the police could do nothing, and they would just think she was crazy. In all actuality, the police would not even care. The situation was bizarre and complicated and strangely related to years earlier, when she worked in Central and South America on assignments. Various sources relayed that someone was out for vengeance.

She said, "I thought you knew things."

Callously, with all harshness and cruelty, he responded, "What I do is not to help or manipulate anything."

The wind was knocked out of Gilda. "Well, chivalry is dead? I have even been told that I was disposable on a few occasions. I have always had to fend for myself!"

His anger erupted. "I do not allow anyone to talk to me that way! Never! Never! You are obviously going through something again! So, good luck, and while you are at it, *lose my number!*"

Gilda interjected softly, "Wow!" Then a scream barreled from her lips. "*You fucking men cannot handle criticism from a woman!* Maybe with my next date, I will first ask that question: 'How do you handle criticism from the female persuasion?'"

Gilda went over again and again the scenario in her mind. She was so thankful she had never slept with Derrick, thus giving him power and ownership over her. He could say nothing but go away with his tail between his legs, screaming his head off that a female could criticize him, a man with God-given attributes of superiority. He believed that women were nothing.

And Derrick Washington hung up on her with a maddening slam of the phone. He   the apparatus on his end. She knew that if he were a man, he would help!

Were women always to have nothing, with no assistance? Nothing…never…never…as Derrick vomited up his manliness. She was stunned and thought to herself, "Why do only men matter?" The reality was that her youth had faded, and she commanded little value in life as a twenty-five-year-old woman. He was probably married, but they had gone out anyway.

There are those who believe strongly in the delusions they have about themselves. The affected cannot handle criticism, and when they have a dose of reality, their entire world tumbles, folding like a house of cards. The mind demands, "I am great! I am great!" The resolution is a lie of omission.

What transpired was just months after a time when Derrick took Gilda out dancing after meeting her in a dive bar. The first thing he said about himself was that he was an intelligence officer, and he was quite gifted.

And he bragged about how he could not believe all the wonderful things that he did—those special endeavors that made him so much better than any other man, and of course all women. If he was a real agent, he would not have uttered a word. She thought maybe this was a sign after all that time of isolation out in the field. There was the inkling even that night that this was just the latest pickup line and that he was really married. That was absolutely not the first time she was lied to. Stephon lied all the time, but sometimes she wanted to believe in those lies as a false sense of hope. She missed James. Anyway, she thought to herself, "I am glad I never slept with him; that would have been a waste of time. Besides, I have already had the best, and he seemed like a pale comparison. So there!" Later, she found out through bar gossip that he was married, but the idea came for the pickup line from an old buddy in naval intelligence.

The burned-out gal thought she would never be a spy again for the rest of her life. She always felt eyes on her and a sense of paranoia. Those were the eyes of people whose job was to take notice and keep tabs. So, the job in the diner was good enough. She welcomed her mundane existence and went about her day-to-day life. Gilda even got a little cat named Rue, whom she babied and loved dearly. Sometimes, she even dressed Rue up in doll clothing, quickly followed by a picture.

One day turned into the next, and another transpired much like the day before. As she turned to food and emotional eating, her waistline grew, and her derriere got extra padding. So, her life drifted into the boring days of daily life. Every day was the same as before. Engaging in conversation with others about her life as a spy had no purpose. She could not ever speak of what she had done. And no one would believe her if she did talk about her clandestine life, and how she was an

expert at shooting guys with their own guns. She would

be labeled crazy and be placed under psychological

treatment. So, the days went on. The dishes were washed,

and the clothing put away. Her life was a toss-up between

ither emptiness or sheer bleakness. Her little cat became

'r best friend. She would often tell her furry little friend

e war stories and her hopes and aspirations.

Perplexed with indecision, she felt that going to

at the diner was the wrong thing to do. She even

ans with a gal she worked with after work. They

ing to the picture show and having a soda

d. On that morning, a knock came at the door.

ght to herself that it was Fred the milkman

me again; he thought she was fair game,

b

did not have a husband to speak of. Fred was

cons

ying to get into her apartment and into her

pants, even though he was a rather unattractive man with rotten teeth. Taking her time, she neared the door and paused. Then there was a soft tapping, not like Fred's desperate banging. She was taken aback and wondered if she should even bother answering the door. Finally, she thought she would just get it over with. On the other side was James Benson, smiling with a sparkle in his eye and asking, "Would you like to go for a ride?"

A yes was delivered without even thinking. She soon noticed that James had come to her door without even bringing flowers. Something in her had chosen to overlook the fact that he was that arrogant; the reality was that he did not have any respect for women, as was the case with most people with the same bigoted perspective. She did not want to face the truth about men in general. Gilda calmed the back of her brain and made the decision to feel the excitement of going out for the day. After all,

James's looks were beyond glamorous, with his jet-black hair and dark, piercing eyes. He was like a dream out of a men's magazine. This was the moment to reconnect with the past. He was someone she could talk to, and he had a defense clearance, so she could converse about her prior espionage work with him. All that time, it had been impossible to relate to anyone. Isolation was a close companion. The girl never compromised herself, because she exclusively felt that it was impossible that this was actually her life. She had for so many years lived an absurd reality. When all was said and done, Gilda was a normal person.

The day commenced at her place. Hours later, James took her out to dinner to one of DC's premier establishments. This was fine dining all the way. Even the maître d' was flirting with her. Yet somehow, she always wanted more out of life, besides being the next hot date on the arm of a debonair gentleman. She came from the backwoods of Romania to army intelligence training mostly because she had a nice ass. Did any of them realize she was a human being? She was exclusively viewed as a sex goddess to be utilized by the intelligence community's endeavors. No one cared.

So, the couple spent the evening reminiscing by making chitchat and trading war stories. He asked as he leaned forward to charm Gilda, "Do you want to get back in the game?"

She responded, "Not really. I was thinking about popping out a baby or two or maybe three. All these years, I have not seen the meaning of life when I have been used by you people and worked like a dog chewing on a rib." The most important point was that he had heard her speak her mind. How else was she to feel, unless she was suffering from a brain tumor? She was fortunate that she did not become a full-blown alcoholic or messed up on street drugs, which were in plentiful supply everywhere, down every crooked street and dead end. She spent her life struggling to have a calm mind.

James leaned forward and asked, "Why are you not grateful that you had such an exciting life? You were a rolling stone with the tenacity and vitality of something greater than yourself. You were the envy of women and desired by men. How great could that be? Look at everything you have done!"

Gilda said, "My life is empty, and in the end, I am alone. Your visit tonight is but one small portion of time. I cannot hold onto this moment, just as the wind rolls across the plains and cannot stay on the ground. Only for the now are we here. Besides, James, as soon as you left me in Sofia, things got strange. Abrasively strange! Most of all, your buddy Stephon was a real control freak, and I do not want to work with him again."

The evening went on, and they returned to Gilda's apartment. He invited himself in, of course. Pulling her in was almost surreal. He kissed her before a moment's glance, and then she melted. They made intense, passionate love. Once again as that transpired between the two, the ground began to rumble. Mountains rose from the ocean. There were tsunami warnings from coast to coast, and the world ceased to spin on its axis. There were even little sparks flying around in the air. That was not bad for an earth-moving experience which was the same scenario as prior encounters because they had really good sex. Somehow the nonsense of that behavior won her over. And James's mission was complete. Their chitchat after having a good time in bed led to Gilda being hooked up as a Pan Am stewardess. She was to continue as an international woman of the world. She was going to fly all over the place and be working a second job as a spy. Yet, this time she demanded a paycheck. She was done with that free nonsense. Foolishly thinking that she would actually be able to spend time with him was a false notion. Maybe that was why she signed up so gleefully.

As James got up, he said, "You have to lose some weight and get that perfect ass back in shape."

Life was hard, yet sometimes people get reprieves that last for a short duration of time and at times extend for longer. She was never Miss Ambitious, but she was now caught up in the whole scenario. Gilda just could not understand the why in the whole matter. She had such a connection with James. The why was that they could be with each other, but espionage was a more seductive bitch. James loved that whore more than any other physical woman. Gilda loved him, and he was always moving on. Why not stay on the ground with both feet planted for more than a moment in time before traversing the world?

Gilda had dreamed of James before she even met him. How many lifetimes would have to pass before he held her in his arms for more than one night? The two had a consciousness that reached beyond time and space. In her dreams, James was that prince in shining armor, but he was never in her presence. He was not there to help or comfort her, but she loved him beyond infinity. James loved her as a beautiful free spirit, but he just could not stay. He was a man on the move, because his energy and projection in life took him to all the places of the world. James had the knowhow to fix anything on the face of the planet. A man of so much charisma could part the seas. He loved Gilda, but he could not be with her because he was a man who did not involve himself in trivial obligations. James was the manliest man and beautiful human being in unison. He loved her, but he walked away for a greater cause, because he was not a selfish person. The things he did were remarkable. What was she to do in life? Was she actually supposed to be with a man she did not want to be with in order to escape loneliness? Gilda only loved James.

Chapter 12

From 1945 through 1946, the discussion began. The debate about forming a new governmental agency for centralized intelligence was widely published in the media. Walter read the newspaper, and once again the journal was slanted toward a governmental agency that would undermine his authority. He grumbled at his desk and crumpled up the paper and tossed it in the waste can. A moment later, he grabbed the paper and unfolded the same journal article he had just read. Cutting the article out, he then placed it in a folder with many other excerpts about the future Central Intelligence Agency. Once again he made a fist, shook it in the air, and mumbled, "Those bastards! I will fix them if it is the last thing I do."

After the war, Walter's organization grew until it was profound and vast. He proudly thought, "This has all been about my level of commitment with running an espionage ring. My organization operated through shell companies, such as vast international businesses like American Express, Chase National, and Philips, the Dutch-based electronics giant. Even one of my top people is a well-known journalist. Most of my operatives are businessmen who travel all over the world. Money is funneled from various sources to pay their salaries to the shell companies. Yet, the vast majority of my contacts are unpaid volunteers. Some people are willing to work for free because of their ideology."

Walter's thoughts were racing. He did not want to lose his position and get thrown out of the game of organizing centralized intelligence. He was blaring. "I will interfere as much as possible. I'll get my people to dig up as much dirt on them as possible and undermine them."

General Sid was one of the main catalysts for instigating the formation of the new intelligence agency. He was well known for running the OSS throughout World War II, and he thought he was going to be the director of the CIA. The Joint Intelligence Committee and the Joint Chiefs of Staff were originally leaning toward the formation of an intelligence committee that would oversee the various intelligences divisions, not a large and all-consuming centralized agency. The committee proposal became rather complex: two subcommittees would be formed, one to oversee positive intelligence, and the other for counterintelligence. He knew that committees could impede production. The notoriety of that progression coming from General Sid caused staggering confusion within the intelligence community and spurred the awareness of the general public—those who were not the elitists of the upper ranks of society. All information (overt, covert, positive intelligence, and espionage) would be funneled into one source. With everything lumped together, there was the question of the functionality and dissemination of designated destinations.

He thought, "Damn them!"

Walter did not favor the creation of the CIA and knew that his organization would no longer have a place in the intelligence community in years to come. He took a proactive stance with advocating against the CIA, although he ultimately knew what was transpiring. In his perception, an underground organization needed to be very discreetly connected to a governmental agency for receiving directives with minimal oversight. Even though Walter ran his organization with what he called shell companies, he was his own authority and did not answer to direct protocol. Part of his struggle and his resentment toward the CIA coming into play was that he would not be the main player in the outfit. He had a certain level of prestige with running the "Organization" which was its own entity. This was as one would have as the head of one's own clandestine empire. His organization went under various names, two of which were "the Pond" and the Universal Service Corporation. These existed during a span of twelve years from 1942 (during World War II) through 1954, during the heart of the Cold War.

The National Security Act of 1947[3] was a milestone for intelligence structuring and stratified organization. This formed the National Security Council, the Central Intelligence Agency, the National Security Resources Board, and the position of the Secretary of Defense for the National Military establishment of the departments of the Air Force, Army, and Navy, all of which had appointed secretaries. The spur to action was the mishandling of information that resulted in the bombing of Pearl Harbor on December 7, 1941. The CIA was established under the NSC. The director of the CIA was appointed by the president and had no restrictions, supervision, control, or other limits to his full reign. The head of the CIA had access to intelligence from all the other agencies. "The Director of the FBI shall make available to the Director of the CIA such information for correlation, evaluation, and dissemination as may be essential to the national security."[4] The CIA had no police or law-enforcement capabilities, however, including the use of subpoenas. "The departments and other agencies of the Government shall continue to collect evaluate, correlate and disseminate departmental intelligence: and provided further, that the director of the

_____

Central Intelligence shall be responsible for protecting

sources and methods from unauthorized disclosure."

Chapter 13

Two days later, after James's departure, Gilda felt ecstatic with him being in DC. With all the attention that he paid to her, she felt truly loved. Yet once again, he was done with her as if he had never been there in the first place. This was nothing but a lie of omission. People lie to themselves all the time. They have pathetic hopes that a situation that did not go in their favor had some value or meaning. The person believing in the meaning of a situation—good, bad, or indifferent—is the one who's stuck in the poor situation in which in the end, they fall short.

Early in the morning, the mail truck pulled up. Squeaking his brakes as usual, the mailman dumped Gilda's correspondence into the mailbox. She was in her kitchen feeding Rue when she heard the mailman's ruckus. She was still in her nightgown, and if she was to go outside to retrieve her mail dressed as she was, she knew her busybody neighbors would see her. She asked herself, "What would the neighbors think? Oh my! The hell with it."

She retrieved her mail, and of course Grace was staring out the front window. She moved toward her door, and Grace said, "Shame on you. No one's husband should have to see you in your nightie."

She just smiled.

Gilda got a letter in the mail from Pan Am. She was in awe about the correspondence and excited to be starting a new job. She felt a reverential mix of fear and wonder. Being a Pan Am stewardess had a certain level of glamour and prestige. Those young ladies were admired. Maybe she could belong to something greater. Yet there was the feeling as if this was another stage of satanic central. The thought was that she needed to bust a move and gain some action with prestige. Yet on the other hand, she was not sure if this was in her personal best interest. At the time, being a Pan Am stewardess was an up-and-coming job for a young woman; besides, those girls exhibited glamour and the air of adventure. Gilda was older than the other airline-stewardess recruits. Apparently, the airline stewardesses were scrumptiously hot in the eyes of men. She made her mind up and dropped twenty pounds within the month. She did this by cutting back on her dinner dates and going for long walks by herself in the morning. There were way too many mornings in which she saw milkman Fred in his truck, watching her with all-intensive eyes. On a lighter note, she got to meet her neighbors and engage in idle conversation. Her appearance began to blossom, and she regained a sway in her hips.

Gilda went out to buy some new makeup, and she bumped into Stephon in the drugstore, and not by coincidence. He was with a young woman named Falcon who was half Gilda's size. She was petite, an itty-bitty little thing. Stephon always loved short women, especially blondes, so he could tower over them and sweep them up by surprise.

Stephon interjected, "I have great news. Falcon is going to Florida with you for Pan Am hostess training. Is that not grand? You have someone you can converse with prior to your training, and you can be the best of buddies."

Gilda faked a grin at Stephon and his skanky friend. "That's spectacular. Wow! I can't wait to make chitchat with her. By the way, what local bar in DC was the grotesque dump where you found her?"

Stephon looked rather pissed off at her accusations that he had a lack of taste in female companionship. He felt that no woman should talk to him in that fashion. Never! Falcon clueless looked around and said in a Southern drawl, "Why don't we get a couple of sodas at the counter? It is a warm, stuffy day."

Gilda had a love-hate relationship with Stephon, who was juggling several girls at the same time as if he was some clandestine pimp. She took too many derogatory comments from him, and he never was anything but emotionally brutal toward her well-being, let alone her personal safety. Stephon was infuriated that none of his girls ever fell in love with him as they did with James.

Stephon was in her life again, and now Falcon, or whatever her real name was, was as well. She found out much later that Falcon's name was Fay O'Connor.

Gilda had lost herself a long time ago. There were always eyes on the ground of sneaky people identifying who's who and what scraps of information they could pick up. At times, she felt paranoid. Even the soda jerk could be working undercover. Her time waitressing at the diner had made her feel that her time was up as a spy, and she was to be moving in a whole different direction in life. She even thought of taking classes at Georgetown University. Oh, the people she would have met and the discussions she would have had with intelligent people would have been such a treat. Going to lectures and watching documentaries would have spurred many conversations. She even would have had picked out the right outfits to wear to school. All those stylist sweaters would have been hers. Her hopes were to be a beautiful young college woman. Unfortunately, she was still in the game, and now she was stuck with Falcon the Southern belle who couldn't give up her real name. The bar was always kept high for her standards; even she had to get ugly in the trenches by lowering the bar.

THE DAY CAME TO GO TO FLIGHT SCHOOL. Gilda did not have to pack much, nor did Falcon. This was because they would be wearing uniforms of one sort or another every day. There would be no going out. That would be out of the question without a chaperon. Gilda was already an independent woman who had lived a life as a spy. Why, at this point of her life, did she need a babysitter to keep herself safe when she had already shot a couple of guys down, some with their own guns? On a lighter note, the clear majority of the girls who worked for Pan Am came from families with old money, and their families needed the assurance. Their daughters would only work a few years before they expected to get married, and arranged scenarios at that. Gilda was lost. She was simply a foreign wild one, and she could very much take care of herself in any situation. No way would she be easily intimidated into falling into the female submissive role. On the same token, the respect that she deserved was never to be had.

As the weeks passed, Gilda's prejudice toward Falcon faded, and she began to think well of her. The gal could hold intelligent articulate conversations. At first, Gilda did not realize what had transpired, but she continued to speak English with her Romanian accent which was now a mélange of a Southern drawl. That was most auspicious and rather bizarre. This stuck with her for years to come.

The two girls started going out on Saturday nights for some stress relief. There was a little dive bar near the training center. One of the flight instructors, Sally, who was extremely married, patronized the bar for happy hour during the week before going home to hubby. The main bar character who resided there was Ludwig Schmidt. He always bought drinks for gals who liked to converse about others' personal information and did not mind keeping their skirts down. Sally was an ongoing source of dialogue, especially about her students, and she loved attention from other men besides her husband. Ludwig copped a feel or two between her legs in the bar.

Ludwig had issues with the female component, especially in occupied Poland. He enjoyed killing women more than throwing babies into the ovens. He had been the assistant to the executioner at Auschwitz. His specialty had been tossing young children into the fires to cook them beside weak victims who were nearly dead and too tired to fight. Even then, Ludwig had drunk like a fish. What was his purpose in life? Ludwig was of a lower note. He had something of a sordid nature.

The war had drawn near a stopping point. The Allies blazed through Germany and went onward toward occupied Poland. When soldiers neared Auschwitz, there was the permeating stench of dead rotting bodies. That was the incarnation of hell on earth. The killing-center enthusiasts got wind that the Americans were approaching. Most cleverly, he got out of that situation by deception and any other means possible.

Ludwig dressed himself in a prison gown and then rubbed dirt and mud on himself. That was a sure cover. Most of the victims who were still alive were so emancipated that they would not expose Ludwig. Everything was falling apart to the Nazi power. Their victims were so close to death that liberation was futile. They were still going to die from the past year of starvation and terror. Beyond help.

Gaining transportation was Ludwig's achievement. He gravitated to Hungary to secure false documents to go to the United States. With money in hand, he was on the move. This man was out to manipulate anyone possible for his own selfish means. The first widow of a fallen officer he found who had money, he would soon marry. Then she would disappear, and he'd make sure before that happened that every document was in his name.

Some activities that Ludwig was involved with called attention to himself; he was helping other war criminals migrate to South Florida. They would have been better off going to Brazil. Using widows, many arranged marriages transpired. The poor unsuspecting gals got stuck with brutes of husbands. The most unfortunate got impregnated, and then they were really trapped.

The Organization took notice of Ludwig, who was really a closeted homosexual with vengeful resentment toward women. He was unlike other men of his stature who embraced their sexuality, resulting in confidence. Seeking the right approach, they looked at their options, which were contingent on whether he was to be brought to trial during a long and drawn-out process, or another scenario would take place. The convincing factor of the danger of this man was when he killed Sally in an abandoned lot, cutting her from one end to the other. Her intestines were left exposed and unraveled upon the ground. He was a predator. That same night, after the deed, he returned to the same dive bar and boasted about how he'd walked Sally to her car to cop a feel.

The night continued as the night before, with stout beer, shots of tequila, and shooting up heroin or cocaine in the men's room, depending on his mood. No one found

Sally's body for some weeks. The Organization knew everything. There was no tip to the police, nor did they do anything to prevent the atrocity. That was not their job.

The girls came in that night. Ludwig bought them drinks as usual, and as always, he got infuriated with the young women's rejection of him. This was because he thought a sixty-five-year-old man was entitled to young flesh, and those girls were supposed to like it. They put up with his ongoing shenanigans. He especially targeted Falcon by being even more insulting and degrading than ever. At times, he could be intelligent and clairvoyant enough to get one to relax, and then he was completely and utterly brutal mentally. It was a real mind fuck.

The door opened, and Falcon took no notice. Then the door closed again. Gilda saw, and went outside. Stephon was standing around the corner waiting. He said,

"This is simple. When Ludwig goes to the men's room again to shoot up, because it is getting late, order another beer and shot for him." Stephon passed her a bag with some power in it. Again, he spoke. "When he is indisposed, put this in his glass, and when he sits back down, pour the fresh beer onto the contents and get him to drink swiftly. He will already be out of it from drinking and drugging all night. He will take the glass without a second thought. Do not get any of the powder on yourself. After he drinks his beer and tequila, wash your hands."

Gilda tucked the bag under her arm and walked back in, bubbly as usual. No one seemed to have taken notice of her absence. Falcon was still sitting there in the same spot, intoxicated and dreading the ongoing sadistic mantra from Ludwig. Then he got twitchy. Getting up from the bar, he headed to the men's room and found a stall. His needle absorbed the contents of a vial. Then the euphoria set in, and he once again was king of the world.

In the meantime, Gilda poured five ounces of sodium hydroxide into his empty beer glass. Sodium hydroxide was used to dissolve the bodies after the mess the Nazis left. That was what she dumped into Ludwig's empty glass. Gilda ordered a fresh bottle of German beer and a double tequila. Ludwig returned, floating through the room. He poured the beer onto the sodium hydroxide concoction, and Gilda said, "Let's get out of here and have some fun." Falcon's face turned pasty white. Her mouth dropped, and she uttered nothing.

In one swallow, the tequila went down and then the beer. The job was done. Ludwig quickly said, "That beer was hot."

Gilda added, "It's hot in Florida."

After that, he could not utter a sound; he simply foamed at the mouth. He was cooking from inside out. That substance seeks water, and every drop was melting him. Ludwig fell off backward from his barstool and seemed to melt from inside out.

Falcon tried to exclaim, quick, someone call a cab, he needs to see a doctor, but Gilda kicked her in the leg.

No one seemed to budge. This could have been for all his time spent there in which he was such a complete ass. They just watched, which was the strangest thing ever. They watched him die.

Gilda nudged Falcon and said, "Let's get out of here. Now!" Then the two returned to the dorms and never spoke of what had just transpired. Nevertheless, Gilda started to realize she was becoming a gifted assassin. Maybe she would go to hell, or maybe there was no hell. The truth was that hell was on earth for those such unfortunate souls.

Two days later, the girls graduated from the Pan Am hostess flight-training class of October 1947.

Chapter 14

After the war, times were different—as if that needed to be explained to Walter. He'd had a lot of financial backing during the war and the following two years. His operation had no budget, and he did not need to answer to anyone. He had free range to conduct an elusive show according to his rank. His guys and gals went everywhere on the face of the planet to perform sneaky maneuvers. They had the front of businesspeople working for major corporations, otherwise defined as shell companies, which are still in this world today. Even the mafia and any other secret organizations had front businesses. This was no new concept, but the skulking behavior was quite efficient to conduct on a level with simultaneously performing other endeavors. A cloak of secrecy was what

Walter gave his people, who were already acclimatized to the work of espionage.

Walter Jones got out of his cab and went inside. The rain soaked his overcoat. He was at a club he frequented and had much association with. At the front desk, Walter was handed a stack of mail that he shuffled through and placed in his attaché case. This was one of his points of contact, even as a civilian. Even after all those years, he still continued to accept clandestine mail drops at the New York Athletic Club on 180 Central Park South. He spent many days there in the various sports rooms and the steam room. That was a place to meet others.

Gilda got off a bus on Central Park South. She wore a business suit, an overcoat, and a man's hat. In fact, she was wearing all men's clothing. Her collar was pulled up, hiding her soft face. A pair of dark-rimmed glasses broke up her appearance. No one on the bus noticed her sex other than a homeless man who could not focus on anyone but her. He even mumbled some deranged statements at her to pick him up as his sugar mama. The homeless man yelled as she got on the street, "Don't go, sweetie! Let's take a power nap together." Everyone wondered at his strangeness.

The time was one in the afternoon. That hour was for laundry service pickup. A truck driver pulled into the alley, grabbed the bags of wet towels, and tossed them in the back of the truck. Gilda waited until the truck was gone, hopeful that this day, the attendant would be too lazy to lock the door to the alley. She walked toward the door with rain dripping from her man's hat. Gilda saw the door was still ajar for success that day, after a few trial runs. As she pulled the door open, she saw a landing with one set of stairs going down and another going up.

Taking the upper route, she climbed quickly. She thought, "Where is Walter? I have to talk to that bastard." This was a men's private club to the utmost extent. Women were excluded unconditionally. There were a few attempted runs when Gilda made the audacious decision to infiltrate a cluster of men.

Gilda had reached the main corridor when an usher asked for her overcoat. She reached into her jacket's upper pocket and pushed a button. A manly sounding recording said, "Do you know where Walter Jones is, my fine man? Please show me the way."

The usher said, "Why yes…yes. Come this way."

Gilda, feeling stressed at this point, followed the usher.

She was thankful that Walter was not in the steam room with the boys. Her glasses would have fogged up, and she would have looked even more out of place.

Besides, she did not really want to see anybody undressed.

Walter was in the salon sipping an afternoon brandy of the finest variety. Deep in conversation, he never noticed the new man come in. In fact, none of the other gentlemen were paying any attention. They were all recuperating from their physical exercise and regrouping with a few cocktails.

She canvassed the room, looking for an easy in. There were none. Yet Gilda looked suspicious in her coat and hat. The first person who focused on her was the bartender, an older gentleman named Larry with silver hair and dazzling smile. Larry kind of smirked but addressed her by offering her a drink. He made her a whisky sour with a twist of lime. Larry said, "You might like this."

Picking up the glass with her soft hands, she held it to her lips and inhaled. The man sitting next to Walter was Harrison, who did not recognize Gilda but greeted the person with a smile. That day there had to have been credit given toward her tenacity.

The focus shifted toward her because she was still in an overcoat and wearing a hat. With suspicion, Harrison gave a how-do-you-do. She gave a small wave and smiled. Taking off the hat, she unleashed her long brown mane. She placed her glasses in her pocket to expose her jade-green eyes as she walked over to the guys, who looked infuriated. A seat was available, so she plopped down as she loosened her jacket. She said, "Well, let me tell you a thing or two about my handler Stephon. I am just about fed up with him. He throws all kinds of sexual innuendoes at me and is constantly insulting me. I feel like I am trapped in this whole scenario, as if I do not have any choice in the matter."

That was basically true. She was trapped, and she had no

respect.

Walter said, rather annoyed, "What do you

propose?"

Gilda replied, "Just talk some sense into

Stephon."

Harrison said, "Well, is that not a rather mundane

complaint?"

Gilda could not believe her ears. Did she not have

the right to state that she was being sexually harassed?

This was completely acceptable behavior for her to

accept. She could not get anyone to intervene for her.

Walter said, "Honey, you have a lot of work to

do. So just get your ass back down to Florida and get on

with your flight-attendant job. We will contact you when

we deem it is appropriate. Do you not understand what I am saying? Do not bother me with this trivial nonsense! This is all a sack of bologna. You have just wasted my time, because you can't keep your feelings in check. That is so typical with women. You girls always navigate according to your emotions, and we men make decisions and conduct ourselves on pure logic. That is what makes your sex weak and makes us the superiors. Just go. Stop staring at me and move along."

She had not even sat there a moment longer before she was escorted out of the men's club. Being ahead of her time was unfortunate for her, because her argument was to no avail. The scene was clever, which was noted by them, but on Gilda's part it was a waste of time. She was sent on her way. Too bad for her. The men went about their conversations of what was to transpire in the world and the grand scheme of things.

INNOVATIVE METHODS OF MILITARY AND INTELLIGENCE approaches were advancing, and techniques were perfected from trial runs. A certain political climate was conducive to the rising of a global spy network. This was when the groundwork was done for the beast to be put into place, which was woven into present-day technological life. Most contacts donated their know-how for idealistic reasons, mainly because they did not receive a paycheck. The vast majority, as the Organizer believed, would never work for the CIA, no matter what. There was a slipping of power, and the Organizer as an independent contractor had lost faith. He foresaw the demise of his network in the near future and in vain tried every possibility to secure his international club. In turn, every possibility he had, he sought to discredit the CIA. Every accusation was dispersed: the CIA agents had no idea about foreign political climates, even though all of them were Ivy League graduates from the finest institutions in the United States and they were from well-established and well-connected families.

Walter invested a lot of energy into being the Organizer of his own international spy endeavor. His power was dissipating, and he wanted to stop the CIA. He desired to hold on to his network of friends. Following the realization that this venture was to be lost, a slew of "dirty linen" reports circulated in order to mock the CIA and at every turn slander it by screaming out incompetency. Any indiscretion they did was enhanced and of course broadcasted to say that the CIA did not have a clue about how a secret organization should operate. Despite all the negativity, the CIA prevailed. Despite the Organizer's slander and fears, the CIA seemed to do all right over the course of time.

Chapter 15

After flight school, Gilda and Falcon parted ways. Falcon
was the first girlfriend she'd had since she was a child.
Life became routine again, with many successful flights.
Yet Gilda missed the stability of when she was a waitress
in DC and trying to have a normal life. This way was
always on the go, staying at uncomfortable hotel rooms
that always needed a good cleaning. She met a whole
community of various sorts of people. Post-flight dating
was common for her and was on the guy's dime. Her
newfound companionships always enjoyed talking about
themselves relentlessly. That was what took over the
conversation. Gilda took up writing her notes in the
ladies' room when she excused herself from the table.
Later she would always finish her reports, to be
redirected to the nearest go-between.

A full year passed. Gilda became an experienced flight attendant. Almost immediately, she got the hang of the job. The job was enjoyable, and life was steady. No one from the espionage community—meaning Stephon—was bothering her.

One day, she got word that the flight that Falcon was working crashed in the mountains of France. The company did not give up much information, nor did Gilda know anything about Falcon's relatives. That only left an empty void in her life, along with many others that already existed. Once again, she was all too aware that she did not have anyone in her life. She was only surviving from event to event, with no comfort. The only destination was the next mountain to climb or the rush from the next adventure.

Strangely enough, Gilda's next assignment was to Paris, France. This was to be a melancholy trip.

Somehow, she was issued a new uniform prior to departure. The morning moved on. The flight was out of LaGuardia, New York. Not even midway through the flight, James was sitting in a first-class seat looking ever so debonair, as usual. She was taken aback with the realization that he was really there. Years had passed since she'd seen him last. Her heart finally began to beat. She was blushing and short of breath. James was undercover as a businessman. The flight went well without much turbulence. James asked if she could meet him for dinner upon arrival at their destination. She was like a young girl, as elated as possible. In her mind, she started to make believe that this was it. It was finally it, although the word "it" has no significant connotation. In other words, "it" does not mean anything at all. As any woman would think, besides putting aside the notion that she was a spy, maybe he was going to truly love her and hold her as if she were his.

A few hours passed, and she rendezvoused with James at a quaint restaurant called Au Coin de la Rue. She had bathed and put on fresh makeup. She smelled sweet like a flower and radiated beauty. Her dress was simple but complementary to her figure. The dinner was superb. James ordered escargot in a whipped herb butter, and then the rack of lamb with a chocolate-jalapeño béarnaise sauce. Gilda had a most succulent filet of halibut in a berry Cajun glaze. The food for both of them was as if the experience was an orgasm in the mouth. That dinner was so good. James asked her questions about her well-being by taking an interest in her. The evening progressed, and the two returned to his chambers not far down the street. He made intense, passionate love to her, tossing her around every which way. Then he said with all sincerity, "I found someone. I have really found true love in my life. She is my heart's delight. This is the type of woman whom I've always wanted to be with. She was a virgin before she met me. I knew that I was destined to marry her, and she is going to have all my children."

Gilda reflected to herself, "What just transpired?" Then she said, "So this woman is now your new soul mate whom you feel this complete and utter bond with? What about me? Was I never your little golden star?"

A long pause followed in her thoughts that seemed to linger into abject confusion.

James interjected, "Are you not happy for me? We are just friends, are we not? Besides, you have no right to criticize me...never...never... You should be grateful for my manliness. I JUST MADE LOVE TO YOU. WHAT ELSE DO YOU WANT."

Gilda screamed with every ounce of her being, "I *am not* here exclusively for your entertainment! You do not even consider me as a human being. You are a selfish bastard. Fuck you…James!"

In disgust, she got up and left. Before she did that, he said, "It is not your place to judge or interfere."

Gilda said, "What?" She just headed out after that. Apparently, he just wanted something for the moment, and she was supposed to be grateful for his manliness. James always took more than he gave. In retrospect, he had no respect for women because they were put on earth exclusively to serve men. As long as, women knew their place, all would be well in the world.

Upon returning to her hotel room, she was stunned that the gal Suzy who shared a room with her tried to ask what was wrong. Gilda said, "This was beyond all words. You are too nice of a person for me to dump this on you. I was a fool, and I thought that he loved me. My heart is broken. The sadness I feel is unbearable. I feel as if I am nothing."

Then Suzy added, "I have had a few dealings with men. I am sorry that you are going through this. Try to get some sleep; we must go to Cairo early in the morning. Sweetie take a hot bubble bath. Just hold your pillow and try to sleep tonight. Men are what they are, and crying is not going to change them. When it comes down to it, they are just cold and selfish."

THE NEXT PART OF THE JOURNEY was from Paris to Cairo, Egypt. That morning, Gilda woke up early, because she hadn't fallen deeply asleep. Only a short span of slumber was interrupted by her clenching on the corner of her pillow. Her roommate pounded on the door to the bathroom a few times to stop her from sleeping in the slower while standing up. An hour later, she finally got dressed. After dressing in her new uniform, the two descended to catch a shuttle to the airport.

The terminal was busy and packed with people. Gilda moved along with care at that point. She arrived promptly on the hour at the gate and greeted the passengers with all hospitality and graciousness. A young European man winked at Gilda while entering the plane. She smiled reluctantly yet did not think much of the flirtation at that time, but her mind was brewing. Gilda's conscience spoke to her: "How sick can one get of being God's gift to men? Too many dates have passed where I just got disgusted with the whole scene. The point being that I don't have a husband. Men think they are entitled to having my body. The reality is that I don't owe any man anything." As Gilda thought this, she just smiled and said, "Hello, welcome aboard."

Takeoff was bumpy because storm clouds were brewing. Once they reached altitude, it was smooth sailing over the Mediterranean. Ivan, the newest and latest passenger, did nothing but flirt with Gilda the entire duration of the flight. Fortunately, Cairo was a short hop from Paris, and she would not have to contend with him for long. Yet he kept trying to get her attention. She finally submitted to meeting him for a drink at the Intercontinental Hotel in downtown Cairo.

So, the flight ended. Gilda went to meet Ivan, who was a dashing, eloquent young man. He seemed to be charged with conversation and ideas. He desperately tried to get her company. He even announced that his father was a diplomat. She agreed to meet him. The two went for a quick drink and then took a nighttime stroll. The short duration turned into an hour or so, with ongoing chitchat.

A rather noisy car came along. Stopping abruptly, two thugs got out and without speaking grabbed Ivan and pulled him into the car. The car sped off for a short distance, and then backed up, parking at an angle. They manhandled Gilda off the street and threw her into the trunk, where she cut her nose and bled profusely. The thugs did not seem to realize that the girl was the objective until Ivan informed them. The directive was never fully read due to laziness. There was a lot of noise in the trunk, in addition to the fumes. She was getting sick, and she vomited on herself. When the car stopped, it was so forceful that she hit both sided of the trunk, knocking the wind out of her. Then the trunk opened, and she was grabbed by the hair and thrown onto the pavement. This was the American embassy in Cairo. They dragged her to the building from across a courtyard that had spooky metal shutters.

The outpost in Cairo was where operatives' covers were known. This piece of real estate had been in use for clandestine activities for years. The building, which had been taken over from the OSS and SSU, was a steel-shuttered, grilled-windowed, padlocked house that had an air of sneakiness. It was within the US embassy compound at 5 Sharie Lazodle.

She thought in a haze, "What is happening?" Her body was already in pain. Into a room with a bright light she went for a duration of time. She realized this was all an Agency gig, but why did they want her? She always exhibited loyalty and did the right thing. She thought at that moment, "What about everything I have done? I must be nothing but a sex slave who got unruly."

She could not understand due to the fact that she worked for the Organization.

Out of the darkness came her boyfriend, whose appearance had somewhat changed. She had shot VonBrutal so many times in her mind, and he just would not die. His hair was long and ratty. Bare-chested, he flexed his muscles. His skin was pasty white, like the Grim Reaper incarnated. He pulled up a chair. VonBrutal looked down at Gilda as a weak, degraded nuisance of a human being. At that point, she was done—really done. He muttered some words in German that translated to "I got a real treat for you."

VonBrutal was a man of few words. He shot her point-blank in the head. Her skull stayed intact but peacefully rested in a pool of her blood. She joined the ugly people; when one was dead, one was dead. Gilda had given the grim reaper the birdy many times whenever she'd barely escaped with her life, but he finally got her in the end. There was no more sidewalk entertainment, as with the man with the dancing monkey he played music for and gave peanuts to.

VonBrutal was a double agent. With that action, he had exposed himself. Gilda was only to be picked up for interrogation. VonBrutal smiled with glee until he was taken over and disarmed. Thrown in a cell, he was to be dealt with later.

Lying on the floor for a time, Gilda started moving her fingers. Her hair was soaked in blood and getting sticky. She quickly realized she was not dead, but she was in much pain. VonBrutal had only grazed her with the bullet, because he was never a good shot when he was drinking. Not much time passed until the room was empty. Everyone had left for the moment. Getting up unsteadily, she was cautious not to make any noise. She heard a loud ruckus in the other room; people were shouting about how the evening had transpired. One guy was yelling about how VonBrutal had gotten a gun. The agents were accusing one another of being incompetent and arguing over who would submit the report. Aware that they were distracted, she walked down the corridor to the steps of the main floor. All of them thought she was dead. Then she scooted out the door to the gate of the embassy. Gilda lucked out: the guard was fast asleep in the guardhouse, with the keys lying on the table. Grabbing the keys was effortless, and she unlocked the gate. It was in the middle of the night, which is why no one took notice of her as she walked the street.

Thinking was tough, because she had a splitting headache. Her hotel room was no more than five miles from where she was. In about two hours, she was at the front of the Intercontinental Hotel. No doorman was posted because of the wee hour of the morning. Upon entering the hotel, she saw the front-desk man, Johnson.

He said, "Good evening." He knew she was injured. Her purse was gone, along with her room key. Fortunately, Johnson also worked for the Organization. He said, "I have a remedy for you." He went into the back room and got his medical bag, a bottle of scotch, and some food. With a concerned expression, he said, "I will escort you to your room. We can look at that abrasion."

Gilda was getting tired. The evening had been just a bit too much. They reached her room, and Johnson had her sit down. He poured her a large glass of scotch and peeled an orange for her. He applied a damp rag to her head to see what the damage was. The bullet had grazed the left side of her head, making a small path through about two inches of her hair. She had a cut on her nose, along with some bumps and bruises. Johnson got some rubbing alcohol and placed it on the wound. Then he used a suture kit to close the abrasion. Without hesitation, he said, "You can wear a flight-attendant hat on the left side of your head when you go back to work tomorrow."

She looked perplexed.

Johnson demanded, "Write your report before you go to sleep tonight, and hand it to me in the morning. I will forward this incident on promptly. Something drastic went on tonight. I can't believe that they are picking up our people on the street."

She considered, "What is wrong with recuperation? I don't want to get onto a plane in the morning, which is only about five hours from now." Once she got her hands to stop shaking, she wrote out the whole sordid evening. Then she was just too tired to sleep, so she merely rested for a couple of hours. Her alarm went off for forty-five minutes. She did not care. Staying in bed was a better option. Then there was a banging at the door. It was Johnson, with a hearty meal. He asked, "Where's the report?"

Gilda said, "On the table." She ate stubbornly as he read what had transpired the night before. Occasionally, Johnson asked, "What is this word supposed to be?"

Apparently, her spelling was messy under the stress of almost getting killed. Annoyed and irritated, she could not deal with his trivial nonsense and chose not to answer him.

Looking at her still-disheveled appearance, he added, "You have twenty minutes to get ready and out the door. Your ride to the airport will be hear shortly. Now hurry up and put a smile on your face."

Smiling was painful in more ways than one. She made sure she did her makeup that morning, putting concealer on the cut on her nose which was now black-

and-blue. There was a small mirror in the bathroom. She went in again and stared at herself in the reflection of what she thought she saw. Her pissed-off expression did not simulate an overly joyous smile. Managing to motivate those facial muscles was more than disgusting to her. Gilda supposed, "Why can I not just disappear and go on with my life?" That was beside the point. Some people are just indentured to other obligations within the course of their lives.

Johnson banged on the door again. "Come on, let's get a move on!" Her eyes were crusty with sleep, and she stumbled for the door. Once she opened the door, he grabbed her bag and escorted her down the stairs. While in the elevator, he handed her an envelope containing a few written sheets. He said, "Read this on the shuttle to Cairo International. Your duties have changed to another destination than returning to Paris. Good luck—you will need it."

In Gilda's mind she wondered, "What the fuck are you talking about?"

Johnson just chuckled as he pushed her into the shuttle and, gentleman that he was, closed the door for her.

The airport shuttle drove off with a zip. Gilda was not the only one there along for the ride. She looked around. There was a woman and another man besides the driver. They both said good morning to her. Frank asked, as he folded his newspaper, "Where are you flying to?"

That was difficult to answer, because Gilda did not know yet. Not being able to respond promptly to that simple question would make her look like a complete idiot. Apologizing, Gilda said, "I am still trying to wake up. There was not enough time to get a cup of coffee."

Frank said, "Yes, Egyptian coffee is excellent. My grandmother makes the best blend. I always love her meals, especially the coffee."

The woman on the van was fat and dumpy and rather prudish in nature who was bloated. Dotty announced, "You must have been out drinking all night. I know how you flight-attendant girls like to party. There is a constant supply of men to buy you free drinks. Am I not right?"

Gilda had been abducted and shot at last night. She just smiled at Dotty and said, "Yes. I was out drinking all night with half the men in Cairo. The boys really *loved* my company. I had the best time ever. I even did more shots of liquor than any of them. The evening was so much fun. They were sad to see me go. You should have been there, because you would have loved it."

Dotty just made a face and decided to look out the window, ignoring anything that Gilda spoke of.

The driver, Mohammed, said, "It will be a glorious day. There is no traffic to speak of, and the skies are clear. Your job will be easy for you today."

Gilda thought, "If he only knew." Her brain was relaying some agitated messages. If she could only let out a scream. Then, maybe for a moment she could have been someone else.

That whole conversation was but a murmur. She was almost in a surreal state of mind, as if these people were painting some distorted circle. Gilda was still in a state of shock and felt like she had gone out of her mind. A strong person can only take so much before they shut down. If she could have just rested a few days with a little tender-loving care, she would have bounced back phenomenally. But no. Johnson just pushed her back into work without any consideration that she was still a human being. He must have thought that he was building character within Gilda. With an attitude, she opened the envelope to reveal the contents, which were all handwritten. The directive went:

Gilda, you have been in our best service by completing your assignments with vigor and tenacity. Your next destination is to fly into the international airport in Lubumbashi, Belgian Congo. You will meet a diamond excavator named Bram Kuiper who dabbles in exporting uranium to the Russians. He will show you around the region, which he does with all his love interests. At that point, you will subtly be contacted by one of our people for your next directive. MOST OF ALL GET ALL

INTEL AND SECRURE DOCUMENTS

by your womanly persuasions!

After Gilda was done reading, she realized what gate she

must get to in order to work. No one on the shuttle paid

any attention to her as she shredded up the paper and

threw it out the window like confetti on a hot Egyptian

day.

It was seven in the morning, and she was sweating

like a fat hog in heat. Gilda worried about all her makeup

running off her face from the temperature. With all her

hurrying that morning, she had overlooked putting on

deodorant. Halfway through the flight, she would be

smelling through perspiration. Putting everything aside,

she was gaining mental preparations for this leg of the

journey. She started to think of what gate she had to get

to, which had not been disclosed in Johnson's correspondence. That would be figured out at the airport, without her looking like a complete idiot.

Even with everything the girl had gone through the night before, her appearance was still rather attractive. This could have been explained by having youth on her side. Back in the day, airline attendants were required to wear high heels while working. That morning she was running, and it took nearly fifteen minutes to find out that she was to be at gate E-9. The clicking of her heels reverberated down the corridors. This gave her the appearance of a cute and entertaining little puppet. The prancing was enhanced by her blue uniform and tight skirt. She never slipped once until she broke a heel and then noticed that she had a run in her pantyhose.

Upon arriving at gate E-9, she found that all the passengers had boarded. The terminal was as hot inside as it was outside. Gilda came running toward the gate with her little heel clicking and clacking. Her tight uniform was about to spilt. Breathless, she was sweating profusely, and her makeup was running. She made an unfashionably late appearance, claiming that there was traffic, which wasn't true. At the time, none of the other Pan Am staff seemed to care. They were just glad she was there. Her assignment was different from the usual; she got to work in first class attending to the elitists.

After takeoff, she commenced serving drinks casually to the few passengers she catered to. Yet her disposition was not rosy and sweet. Most of the time, her hands were shaking, and she spilled the passengers' drinks on them and they were quite perturbed. This went on until she allowed herself to swig a couple of single-serving bottles of vodka. After that, she seemed to manage, except for smiling and being well-rounded in her socially acceptable graces. As she served, she politely asked their names until Bram Kuiper announced himself and said, "Gilda." She smiled and went about her tasks.

Africa is a very large landmass, so the flight from Cairo to Lubumbashi was a long stretch. Most of the passengers dozed off except Bram, who sipped on his martini as he swished the olive around. He was a diamond miner by trade but picked up extra currency and favors in the espionage field. There was his sneakiness with selling uranium. Bram said, "My, what are we going to do with you?"

Gilda just looked at him as if she were sick and tired of this whole underground sexist scenario. If she could have just jumped out of that plane at the very moment to parachute to a new location, she would have. She missed her simpler life when she'd worked at the diner. The same people came in every day and ordered the same breakfasts. Most of all, she missed her cat Rue, and how happy the little kitty was to see her when she got home. She hated having to give Rue to her neighbor when she went back to work. When she did, the cat looked at her with the saddest eyes. Even at that time, she knew that had not been a smart idea. She'd had an inkling of what was to come. The life of adventure would have its price to pay.

Gilda responded to Bram's sexist remark. "It is not your place to do anything with me. What work are we going to be doing? I am not doing anything for your personal entertainment. Can we have an understanding?"

Bram look undignified and even grunted, "Eh." Then he said, "Meet me after the flight. I will come by your hotel after you change; take a shower, because you already need one."

Gilda knew that his spitefulness was due to his bruised ego and because he really wanted her.

Once the passengers left the plane with their belongings, the local Pan Am representative approached Gilda with a serious look. Jill Carter was not the kindest of people of Pan Am human resources. She stared and laughed at Gilda for a moment. Clipboard in hand, she began to list all of her infractions, including being late for the flight that morning. Jill added that Gilda's uniform was not in pristine shape and her hair was not done to standard. Jill said, "Contingent upon your conduct, we are letting you go. You will not have any more employment with us. We have no obligations to you at this point. You may now leave." The expression on Jill's face was that of an evil uncaring sort. She was enjoying every moment of terminating this flight attendant. That was one of her favorite things to do. Then Jill ripped the wing pin off of Gilda's uniform.

Gilda was stunned. This woman was derogatory and insulting beyond belief. Then Gilda asked, "What, am I at least getting a flight back to the States?"

Jill said with a smirk, "No, Pan Am has no obligations to you. What do you not understand? Now, I have other business to attend to. Stop looking at me like that. Just go on your way. We do not owe you anything. It was in your contract that we can dismiss you for infractions. You have really pushed things to the limit by nearly missing several flights. At your age, you should have been more self-conscious."

Gilda said, "What do you mean 'at my age'? I'm only twenty-seven!"

Jill, with an evil little expression, informed Gilda that she was considered old for a flight attendant and was past her prime. "Pan Am only wants young women to work for them." Then Jill added, "You need to find yourself a man before it is too late. You look old and haggard."

This was obviously another manipulative joke set up by the Organization to make her work overtime and to focus on more resourceful possibilities as a spy. Her pocketbook was going fast. She had no money, and now no job. She was stuck in the Congo with contending with Bram, whose front was that of a diamond miner but who had connections in the uranium fields.

Gilda really did not want to play this game anymore. Maybe she had just been fired because of her poor work performance as a flight attendant. She did fall asleep during the flight when she was supposed to have been working. It was difficult working two jobs, especially with what had transpired in Cairo. Still, at that time, she could not figure out why the Agency had picked her up or how she had gotten out of the embassy compound so easily. There had to have been some sort of incompetence on their part or maybe not.

Gilda had the most pathetic thought: "Oh, this is to help me develop as a human being. Oh my! I am so grateful for this living experience with the CIA." She thought this full of disgust and cynicism.

So, Gilda slowly walked out of the airport terminal. When she got to the front of the building and was standing on the sidewalk, she looked at the cabs. Then she looked again. There were no options that she could wrap her mind around. Once again, she heard the echo in her brain that she was nothing but a sex slave. That was when she decided to bolt. Gilda thought, "There have to be kind people in the world who will help me."

There was one lonely cab at the end of the line—a VW Bug that was more than broken down. The cab driver was the poorest of the lot. Gilda leaned through the window and said, "Can you help me?" Tears poured through her eyes. She was tired and hyperventilating. Once again, she said, "Please."

The driver was named Adisa, which translated to "lucid one." He said, "Please get in."

All she had on her was her Pan Am uniform and a change of clothing in the bag she carried which was another uniform and clean panties.

Chapter 16

Some time passed once the authorities' realization was made that Stephon was falsifying his reports to the holding house because Gilda had rejected his affections. He even slandered her to James to make her look unseemly. Gilda was made to be portrayed in a dismal light by Stephon, where she would be investigated by the Agency. Nevertheless, she was disposable, and a new, hotter agent would take her place. All secrets died with her, did they not because Gilda was classified as DISPOSABLE?

What happened to Gilda was such a setup. Money was even transferred to a Swiss bank account that was supposedly in her name. Sometimes in life there is nothing one can do when everyone else has an alibi that is stacked against the inflicted.

Stephon was never disciplined. He was always above the rules, mostly because his family had money and connection. There are different rules for different people. This guy could actually go about life doing and saying whatever he wanted, with no repercussions. Nothing ever bothered him for long, because he would simply take another drug and contemplate how great he was. Always, he thought about all the amazing things he had done over the course of his lifetime. Most of all, he was proud of his magnificent good looks, although the years of substance abuse and the massive amounts of alcohol had bloated his body. He still saw himself as a young man. No one could ever criticize him. Shutting them up immediately, he would take offence that they would have the audacity to say anything to him. Some people believe so strongly in the delusions they have about themselves that it is impossible for them to accept censorship. Anyone who said anything to him was met with his nasty callousness. He would let them know in turn that they were below him. As it went, no disciplinary actions were taken against Stephon. One reason was because of who his family was. Another reason was that Gilda was female and thus of lesser value than a male agent.

Stories make espionage out to be some glorious occupation, when in reality the spy's life is a two-headed monster consuming agents from all angles although this beast is a beautiful monster—an enchanting, magical temptress for whom one loses one's soul and very being. Thus, throughout the duration of that damned person's life, the spy is consumed and gobbled up and in the end disposed of. Never are they to utter a word of their secret work. When they die, their idealism is fully intact. Why would anyone forfeit one's life in order to keep a secret?

Adisa and his wife took Gilda in for a time. This was not for long, because people would be looking for her, and their neighbors would see her. The meals were well prepared, and the conversation was refreshing. Politics and spirituality were Adisa's favorite topics. Adisa said, "You are wondering what you are going to do next."

"Yes, I don't have papers to travel with."

Adisa added, "In this part of the world, some people are privileged, depending on their race. You can get by until you find your final destination."

Gilda said, "Oh."

Adisa said with all seriousness, "Just start walking. You are in one of the most magnificent parts of the world. This is a paradise although our land is under fire. People do not have to buy food, because fruit trees are in abundance everywhere one looks. Go see Mosi-oa-

Tunya, otherwise known as Victoria Falls, which no one knew existed until white people discovered that powerful natural wonder. This wonder is between Zambia and Zimbabwe. Most of all, climb Kilimanjaro. You will find God there and will be able to stand at his level. You should simply view our abundance of wildlife. You have to start a new journey in life. I understand the trouble you got yourself into with those people, who have no shred of kindness or compassion. You did not even have to say a word when you got into my cab. I understood your situation. This is a gift from God. You do not ever have to go back to the obligation that controlled you."

Gilda questioned Adisa, "Why are you helping me?"

Adisa said with all seriousness, "I could say I am helping you because I am a man of God, but that is not the reason. Those people you were involved with use people until they are nothing. Is someone really supposed to keep a secret when faced with death and torture? My brother Attu got mixed up with espionage. Attu disappeared. I believe him to be dead. My wife, Gabriella, helps care for his children, because Attu's wife was also killed. My dear, you can still have a life. All you need to do is start walking. There is no problem with getting a ride or people taking you in for the night and feeding you. You are a beautiful human being, and I hope you come to see that there is so much goodness in the world. You made the correct steps; you walked away from that obligation."

Gilda felt relieved. After dinner, Gabriel gave her some clothing to change into. There were many donations from the States, but the clothing was worn, and there were many gaping holes. Anything Gabriel got from donations, she had to stitch or patch up. She picked out a couple of items that were in better condition to give to Gilda. She also gave her a pair of handmade sandals. They would be good for walking.

Gabriel said to Gilda, "Just enjoy being in Africa. There are so many amazing wonders for you to see. This continent is massive. You are a beautiful young woman. Maybe you can meet someone and have a good life. As I believe in God, I believe good things are to transpire for you."

Gilda had had so many people around her for so long who were atheists that she found Adisa and Gabriel refreshing. She was moved, and for the first time in her life she felt unconditionally loved. Being accepted and understood was something she thought she would never have. Yet in the morning, she had to get a move on. They would come looking for her.

Everyone woke up when the rooster crowed, including Gilda. Gabriel prepared breakfast as the rest of the house got situated. Their life was simple and basic. They were the kindest people she'd come upon in years. The meal of spicy lentils and eggs was different. Before they were done eating, an older woman named Ada came to their home. She brought Gabriel a dead chicken for their dinner. The old lady was a very powerful medicine woman.

Ada said, "A fair one has shown up. She seems as if she wants to disappear, but because she is so pale, that would be difficult here. Who is she trying to fool? Of course, her people are going to come looking for her, except for the man she loves, who does not love her at all. Do you know how many people she has killed? I tell you, she has brought bad luck on your household."

Adisa seemed to be looking into the distance with a blank expression on his face. Then he took a bit of his lentils and eggs. Continuing to eat his breakfast, he chose not to respond to Ada. Gabriel engaged in conversation with Ada and thanked her for the chicken which they would have that night for dinner. Then Gabriel served Gilda some food. Ada looked at her with the evil eye. Soon the medicine woman moved on.

Soon afterward, Adisa encouraged Gilda to move on as well. Gabriel packed some food into a handwoven backpack and gave her a straw hat. They said their goodbyes, and the day began. She felt uncomfortable imposing on Adisa and his family. As she walked away, she felt sadness for having to leave. This was mostly because they were good and hospitable people.

Down the red-clay road she roamed. A few miles into her trip, she was no longer being passed by any cars.

Being in the middle of nowhere was awesome. Gilda yelled at the top of her lungs, "Wahoo!" Then she took off her hat. She had never felt so free. She walked along in awe of life.

This continued until she heard an oncoming rumbling and saw dust being kicked into the air. Gilda was hoping this was just a fruit truck she could get a lift from. The racket and soot cloud came nearer and nearer. She hoped the truck would just pass, but she was a white girl along the side of the road in the Belgian Congo, and she knew she would draw attention. She got off the road as far as she could. Then the truck came to a screeching halt. She smiled and waved slightly, thinking to herself, "This might be good, or this might be very bad."

The dust seemed to swirl around and overtake the truck. When the air cleared, Gilda walked to the passenger's window. There was no one in the truck. She opened the door. Still no one. Now she got scared. There was a sound of someone relieving himself along the side of the road. Gilda looked over at a man. It was James.

James said, "I have been meaning to talk to you. I really do not think you should get out of the game just yet. You are a very talented agent. Maybe you should reconsider your delusions. What is it that you are looking for? Come on, Gilda, just snap out of it. Whatever is going through your brain, just let it go. You will be better off."

Gilda looked at James. Then she turned and kept walking. He followed her with the truck for a few miles. He stopped, and she got in.

She asked, "You really do not love me, do you?"

James looked away.

The answer was clear, just as Ada had said. Down the road, James stopped the truck to talk to Gilda. Without hesitation, she jumped out and kept going. This time he did not follow her. She knew that she was not truly alone in the world as in reality everyone else is. At this point, she had to make something out of nothing which was hope. Who could blame her? Deception was part of her life in all aspects. The simple day-to-day things are conducive to happiness. If only she'd had the love and support that everyone needs, her life would have been so much better. Out into the great unknown she went, because there was always hope in life. Gilda kept walking with a light in her heart.

Chapter 17

Gilda walked peacefully. She saw vultures flying overhead and smelled the stench. After another mile she saw the damage. There was a pit full of bodies hacked, mutilated and left for dead. Her movements were slow as she stared at the carnage of what had happened to the locals. Stunned, tears ran down her face. The heaviness of the rotting bodies seemed to linger on her clothing. She could not breathe and then vomited. Moving down the road was the only option as the next three to four miles passed. A rumbling came upon her of loud pipes with fire spitting out the tailpipes. She contemplated, "why would there be bikers in the Congo?" They were riding fast, the dogs of Hell, as they convened onto her location. Dirt kicked out into the dryness of the air.

Afraid to look over her shoulder, was what she did.
Gilda was memorized by their moxie let alone the
manliness they projected. At that point, she was trapped.
Her freedom lasted less than 48 hours.

Indian and Monte rolled slowed down and rolled
up to Gilda even more slowly because she kept her back
turned. She smiled out of relieve because she always
liked Monte. The objective was once again overwhelmed
by Monte's manliness.

Indian said, "Do you really want to keep
walking?"

Gilda, "What?"

Monte smile with all moxie and looked over her
sexy grungy body. He gave her a profound look along
with an intense disposition of authority. He annunciated
himself, "what are you doing with your life Gilda?"

Gilda screamed, "it's my life and leave me alone."

Indian, "you will not last three days out here. Are you fucking stupid? Why were you even talking to Adisa? People that are positive cannot comprehend adversity, or what needs to be done in the world. You might of well get your tap shoes out and do a song and dance routine as that amazing Broadway performance."

She seemed as if she was going to cry because once again Gilda was easily offended, yet at that point she just wanted to get on the back of Monte's bike. So, she did with the weight of her pelvis against his back side. As they rode, Gilda noticed how he had the disposition of tapping on his pipes with his hard toe leaver boots. The enigmatic movements were in pace to synchronized travel from both to heaven and hell and then back.

Monte said, "this is still a man's world and you need to be my passenger. Now hold on."

So, she did. The boys and the passenger rolled. Towards Bram Kuiper's Likasi mine. The ride was hot and airy as the Sun had the audacity to set at 5pm. The darkened ride continued with all inviting sweetness. Gilda was very aware of Monte and he was aware of her because she could not identify with other people. They stop short of the encampment in order to silence the bikes and have a quick snack of booze and fruit.

Monte pulled out a duffel back from his right saddle bag, and said to Gilda, "put every file and scratch of paper notation in this bag. We will walk you to the edge of the camp, but beyond that point you only have ten minutes to secure the documents or we are leaving without you."

Her jaw dropped. She thought, "why can't they depend on other girly-girls. Why am I the only female in the scene?"

Indian firmly said, "girl just get your shit on! We are not going to tell you what you want to hear. If you think that because it is obvious you want to be on your way. Yes, there are other's that have an easier way in life. That is not for you. Now, work."

The three of them walked quietly to the base camp which was not well lit, and the terrain was rough with plenty of rocks to trip over. In the shadows, she was still in sandals while she grasped the duffle bag as she went ahead of the boys. Then she had the crazy notion to take off her clothing and walk into to the camp in her buff. Her perfect figure was etched out in the moonlight. Her body was bathed in the darkness with divine highlights. She commenced towards the main trailer which had to be Bram's. He had a light on, and the movements were noted. The unlocked door opened when he came outside for a cigarette. Bram was before his time for the notion of only smoking outside only. Perplexed, he was stunned by the naked flight attended, and he asked, "what is transpiring beautiful."

Gilda said, "I am here to steel all your documents, and then kill you. You must see the humor in that. Please give me a cigarette now, and then some scotch."

Bram noted her honesty and smiled. He said, "come in sweetheart because he did not believe her."

The boys were watching from a short distance, and gasped, "What? Did that bitch actually say that?"

Indian said to Monte, "Are we really going to have to do this NOW?"

Monte nodded, and his facial expression was of disappointment. The two disrobed simultaneously transformed when dropping onto all fours. Their teeth became elongated, and the men had the appearances of four-legged hairy beast. They seemed to scurry about as they neared Bram's trailer. They snarled and snapped their jaws outside. Gilda was on her way of finishing her cocktail and Bram even let her smoke a cigarette inside because he was admiring her fluffy pussy. This was mostly in regards he dared not to go outside. In the vicinity, the mine workers had already meandered home. The armed guards had eaten dinner and were sleepy with full bellies from the campsite. That was the incentive for the lack of pay.

Bram disclosed to Gilda because he was a man that loved to brag for making a profound impression on young beautiful women. He said, "we are going to shut down the whole Belgian Congo in regard to the locals. We have found of way of poisoning them in such a way that resembles the most horrible disease ever. The ill-fated would have the internal organs liquify and they would bleed out of every orifice. Death would transpire in 48 hours or less. There would be no cure for this disease. That would clear this region of any local and international curiosity because foreign medical workers would also fall ill. We just do not have the name for this infliction yet. In time, this man-made disease will terrify the entire plant."

Gilda responded, "oh."

Then Bram pored her another cocktail with a casual smile on his face. He winked at Gilda with an arrogant smirk. Then all Hell broke loose as the naked subhuman men-wolves busted down the door of Bram's trailer. Bram was torn to shreds with his throat being ripped out first. Indian and Monte then lost their magic. And, Indian yelled at Gilda, "you had ten minutes. How lazy of an agent can you possibly be? What the fuck bitch!"

For a moment, she was meek. She grabbed the duffel bag and proceeded to stuff numerous documents into the sac along with little scraps of paper that contained clandestine notation. The men did not know what she heard. At that point, she was working for a greater cause.

Monte just said, "women are like that. You just took her own sweet time. Let's get the girl out of here. Grab the bag from her. Do you remember where we left our clothing."

Indian, "yeah sure."

Monte, "we have less than 90 seconds. Let's go. Although, I have to say something. Does she not look good? I could bend her over and take her right now."

Indian, "Monte, get your head back in the game."

Monte shrugged his shoulders, and grabbed Gilda by the arm, and escorted her out. They moved like a supernatural wind grabbing their clothing and moving back to the motorcycles. When the whole seen transpired there was a strange humming in the air. They rode naked until five miles had passed where upon they dismounted. During the short ride Gilda was pressed up against Monte's nakedness. He felt her. Stopping abruptly, she got off the back of his bike for not more than three steps and he grab her by the torso and mounted her. He was curled over in ecstasy as his member was in her warmth. Taking his time, he thrusted her profoundly.

Indian said, "really? You got to be kidding me. We got to get out of here and finish the job. Gilda is not the job. So, let's get a move on."

Monte acted as if he did not hear Indian. His pleasure was worth that moment in time. Alongside the red clay road, he fucked himself into her being.

Indian, "Get your clothing on. We are out of here."

Gilda was wiped out. Indian said, "make sure the bitch does not fall off the back of your bike! Pay attention! We got to deal with VonBrutal later, and she is going to smell like you. This has been good so far. We have the documents."

Monte, "That was a good show. We need to get to the landing strip!"

Gilda, "what?"

Indian, "yeah, the Bomb Lady is going to pick us up."

Gilda, "really. "What? Is she friends with VonBrutal?

Indian, "yes."

Gilda, "that bastard."

Monte, "notwithstanding your regards to me and him, we got to go!"

Gilda, "I got to get my outfit on."

Indian, "more ways than one. You are such a little girl."

Gilda, "what, do not call me a little girl. I am not one of those."

Indian, "just get your fucking clothing on."

Once again, Indian yelled at Monte, "come on! I can hear the Bomb Lady flying in. We got to go. Do you understand what I am saying?"

Monte, "ok."

Gilda, "ok."

The three with Gilda as a passenger rode fast and furiously to the landing strip which was nothing more than a goat path. The elite state of the ark camouflaged Russian plane landed beyond believe and with accurate precision in the abject dark. The pilot stopped on a dime and rotated the plain and dropped the back hatch so that the bikes were able to drive into the cargo hold. As soon as Natacha VodkaBitch passengers were inside; the hatch was shut that passage were in control central. Natacha came out of the cockpit. She was in her flight suit which was unzipped and her double DD's bulging out. As she greeted fair acquaintances and good tidings, Natacha motioned them for them to utilize the seat belts. The lady was getting a move on fast because there were predictors in the vicinity.

In the limited space, she took off with intended purpose by clearing every land obstacle. This woman knew her plane as well as she knew the POS crop dusters, she flew during WWII to bomb Nazi Germany. She had too because she wanted to stay alive and be able to go home to her children excluding her husband in Southern Russia. Natacha had a refined mind. Maybe that was survival, or maybe that was that she operated under the super national realm. She had accuracy under the command of what targets. Given the responsibility of team leader she guided other female bombers to success which of course they did. They added in the pushing back of the Nazis. Night witches were coined and name because the women aviators had that black magic, and that they were deadly foes.

Yet, Natacha was the kindest and the most compassionate person. War was waging. People defended themselves. When on her missions, her husband cheated on her of course with other women with double DD's that reminded of him of her because she was not there for his consortium. As most men do, they tell their secrets under intimacy. One night when she got the kids out, she though a makeshift bomb with much gun powered and gave a gentle toss into the love chamber and blew him up. She smiled as "the walk" out of the house which was on fire. Within 45 minutes Natacha was confronted by the local KGB to be under employment. Her children were removed to a safehouse, well taken of and loved. All three of them reached scholastic heights and progressed on university standards while Natacha conducted in the realm of clandestine activity. Peace of mind, she was better for the best. Precision was the target while her loved ones were taken care of. Beside all, she was a natural beauty, and beyond intelligent. Her skin was milky white. She had long jet-black hair and eyes of jade. Her figure was perfection.

That day in the Congo plane, she greeted Gilda with compassion because Gilda fell off the back of Monte's back as he abruptly entered the cargo plane. Gilda so painfully met the metal flooring of the plane. She did not have to say anything beside the scene was absurd. Natacha gave a million-dollar smile.

Natacha said, "come sit with me in the cock pit while the boys stay in the back with their motorcycles. There is a long fur in the closet for you. When we take off the temperature is going to drop. You sweet thing, everything is going to be alright. Trust me."

As confused as she was Gilda uttered, "that is all good."

Natacha had the utmost skill as she took off curtailing the rouged terrain. Into the air was another well-known realm to her. In the cockpit both of the ladies were wearing Russian furs. The two talked women to woman. That was the genre of conversation that men were not privileged to hear. The ladies smiled and laughed with all of their intense focused conversations. Then Natacha turned on the music which sounded of an American Western from the bad lands. The sounds followed by American Indian realms and beats as a preparation for war. The music was followed by string instruments especially the cello.

Gilda asked, "where are we going."

Natacha, "into the great unknown."

Gilda's eyes grew heavy, and she slipped onto slumber as the boys routed around in the cargo hold.None of the passengers knew where they were going. They were going somewhere by flying East for another adventure.

Conclusion of Book One of the VonBrutal Series

Bibliography

"1641 Files to 1641 File; 1641 Files," 1945–1946; ARC ID 4509737, entry 16. Grombach Organization ("the Pond"), Record Group 263, records of the Central Intelligence Agency. National Archives, College Park, MD.

"Harmful Influences against Forces of Anticommunism," p. 1, folder 1, box 11, Record Group 263, records of the Central Intelligence Agency, p. 12, ARC ID 4509733. "Greek Intelligence to Iraq," p. 2, Grombach Organization ("the Pond"), subject and country files 1920–1963. National Archives, College Park, MD.

"History of the Army Special Intelligence Branch," Record Group 263, records of the Central Intelligence Agency, p. 12, ARC ID 4509733. "SOP (Field) to Soviet Artillery in the Offensive," Grombach Organization ("the Pond"), subject and country files 1920–1963. National Archives, College Park, MD.

"National Security Act of 1947: July 26, 1947," public law 253, eightieth Congress, chapter 343, first session, s. 758.

"Please Return to Lt. Col. J. V. Grombach Room 2E 740 Pentagon Building," Record Group 263, p. 12, ARC ID 4509733. "SOP (Field) to Soviet Artillery in the Offensive," the Grombach Organization ("the Pond"), subject and country files 1920–1963. National Archives, College Park, MD.

"Report on Intelligence Matters," background material to clippings re: government personalities, Grombach Organization, records of the Central Intelligence Agency, entry 12, Record Group. 263, National Archives, College Park, MD.

"Top Secret OSS Report," p. 4, folder "Monogram on OSS 1942–1945," box 18, p. 12, Record Group. 263, records of the Central Intelligence Agency, ARC ID 4509733. "Greek Intelligence to Iraq," Grombach Organization ("the Pond"), subject and country files 1920–1963. National Archives, College Park, MD.

Transcript of the Marshall Plan (1948), www.ourdocuments.gov (accessed March 10, 2016).

"US Tells the World Its Plans," container 6, subject and country files 1920–1963, entry 12, records of the Central Intelligence Agency, Record Group. 263.

Made in the USA
Middletown, DE
21 March 2020